The Garden
with Seven Gates

Concha Castroviejo in 1980, Madrid. Photo courtesy of María
Antonia Seijo Castroviejo.

The Garden
with Seven Gates

by
Concha Castroviejo

Translated from the Spanish by
Robert M. Fedorchek

Introduction by
Carolina Fernández Rodríguez

Lewisburg
Bucknell University Press
London: Associated University Presses

Associated University Presses
2010 Eastpark Boulevard
Cranbury, NJ 08512

Associated University Presses
Unit 304, The Chandlery
50 Westminster Bridge Road
London SE1 7QY, England

Associated University Presses
P.O. Box 338, Port Credit
Mississauga, Ontario
Canada L5G 4L8

The paper used in this publication meets the requirements of the American National Standard for Permanence of Paper for Printed Library Materials Z39.48-1984.

Library of Congress Cataloging-in-Publication Data

Castroviejo, Concha.
  [Jardin de las siete puertas. English]
  The garden with seven gates / by Concha Castroviejo ; translated from the Spanish by Robert M. Fedorchek ; introduction by Carolina Fernández Rodríguez.
    p. cm.
  Contains a dramatic version of the short story Garden with the seven gates.
  Includes bibliographical references.
  Contents: We have the stars — Blas's dream — The country that had no birds — The sparrow and the moon — A mermaid and a magistrate, 500 neighbors and a singing blackbird — Matías the half-wit — The year that fell into the sea — The weaver of dreams — The pirates of The terrible one — Martolán, apprentice Magus — Barú and the giant — The conceited buzzard — The little girl and the sea — Karlantán and prince Atal's pearls — The garden with seven gates.
  ISBN 0-8387-5559-3 (alk. paper)
  1. Children's stories, Spanish—Translations into English. I. Title: Garden with 7 gates. II. Fedorchek, Robert M., 1938– III. Title

PZ7.C268744413 2004
862'.64—dc21

                                                                    2003057700

PRINTED IN THE UNITED STATES OF AMERICA

Other Bucknell University Press Books
Translated from the Spanish by Robert M. Fedorchek

- Palacio Valdés, Armando. *Alone and Other Stories.* 1993.
- Pardo Bazán, Emilia. *The White Horse and Other Stories.* 1993.
- Picón, Jacinto Octavio. *Moral Divorce and Other Stories.* 1995. In collaboration with Pedro S. Rivas Díaz. Introduction by Gonzalo Sobejano.
- Bécquer, Gustavo Adolfo. *Legends and Letters.* 1995. Introduction by Rubén Benítez. Drawings by Jane Sutherland.
- Alarcón, Pedro Antonio de. *The Nail and Other Stories.* 1997. Introduction by Cyrus C. DeCoster.
- Caballero, Fernán, Antonio de Trueba, and Pedro Antonio de Alarcón. *Death and the Doctor: Three Nineteenth-Century Spanish Tales.* A Bilingual Edition. 1997. Introduction by Lou Charnon-Deutsch.
- Alarcón, Pedro Antonio de. *The Nun and Other Stories.* 1999. Introduction by Stephen Miller.
- Alas, Leopoldo, "Clarín." *Ten Tales.* 2000. Introduction by John W. Kronik.
- Picón, Jacinto Octavio. *Sweet and Delectable.* 2000. Introduction by Noël Valis.
- *Stories of Enchantment from Nineteenth-Century Spain.* 2002. Introduction by Alan E. Smith.
- Valera, Juan. *Doña Luz.* 2002. Introduction by Beth Wietelmann Bauer.

For Rebecca,

Who has already woven dreams of her own

Contents

Translator's Preface

EVERY READER OF Charles Perrault and the Brothers Grimm knows that fairy tales are not for children alone, inasmuch as they speak to fantasies and fears that are our constant companions in life. The stories that make up *The Garden with Seven Gates* (El jardín de las siete puertas, 1961) by the Spanish author and journalist Concha Castroviejo (1910–95) will, I believe, be viewed in the same light—although peopled with children protagonists, they are not for children alone.

There are, to be sure, narratives that qualify as latter-day fairy tales. "The Weaver of Dreams" will strike a chord with every adolescent girl who has suffered ridicule, and recalls the torment of ridicule. There are morality tales, like "The Conceited Buzzard" and "A Mermaid and a Magistrate, 500 Neighbors, and a Singing Blackbird." There are lyrical pieces like "Martolán, Apprentice Magus," cautionary tales like "The Little Girl and the Sea," and enchanting pieces like "Karlantán and Prince Atal's Pearls." And there is one of the most evocative tales to be found in modern Spanish literature of the mutual love of a grandson and grandfather in "We Have the Stars." In a word, the stories of *The Garden with Seven Gates* are a sensitive representation of the minds, joys, fears, and sorrows of children as depicted by a wise, insightful writer. The book is capped by the minidrama "The Garden with Seven Gates," the title piece in dialogue, which shows that the richest of imaginations are truly unplanned journeys of the mind.

In addition to *The Garden with Seven Gates*, which received the Spanish publisher's first Doncel Prize for Stories in 1961, Castroviejo wrote several other books for children: *The Pirates* (Los piratas, 1962), *The Buzzard* (El zopilote, 1962), and *Lina's Days* (Los días de Lina, 1971). In long fiction she published two novels: *Those Who Went Away* (Los que se fueron, 1957), about Spanish Civil War expatriates—a widow and her son—who go first to Paris and afterwards to Mexico, where the mother sees that her son's future is there, not Spain, and *Eve of Hate* (Víspera del odio, 1959), about a woman who has an illegitimate child and grows to hate her husband for his cruelty and greed, again with the Spanish Civil War as background.

I am very grateful to four people: María Antonia Seijo Castroviejo of Madrid, Spain, daughter of Concha Castroviejo, for having given me permission to translate her mother's work; Minia Bongiorno García, of Santiago de Compostela, Spain, who located her, thereby allowing me to initiate a correspondence with her; Carolina Fernández Rodríguez of the Universidad de Oviedo, Spain, for having written the introduction; and my friend and colleague Consuelo García Devesa, who guided me through a number of linguistic challenges.

I used the second edition of *El jardín de las siete puertas* (Madrid: Doncel, 1968) for the translation.

Original Titles

Tenemos las estrellas / We have the stars

El sueño de Blas / Blas's dream

El país que no tenía pájaros / The country that had no birds

El gorrión y la luna / The sparrow and the moon

Una sirena y un corregidor, 500 vecinos y un mirlo cantor / A mermaid and a magistrate, 500 neighbors, and a singing blackbird

Matías el tonto / Matías the half-wit

El año que se cayó al mar / The year that fell into the sea

La tejedora de sueños / The weaver of dreams

Los piratas de «La Terrible» / The pirates of *The Terrible One*

Martolán, aprendiz de mago / Martolán, apprentice magus

Barú y el gigante /Barú and the giant

El zopilote presumido / The conceited buzzard

La niña y el mar / The little girl and the sea

Karlantán y las perlas del príncipe Atal / Karlantán and Prince Atal's pearls

El jardín de las siete puertas / The garden with seven gates

Biographical Profile: Concha Castroviejo

María Antonia Seijo Castroviejo

CONCHA CASTROVIEJO was born in 1910 in Santiago de Compostela, into the bosom of a family of intellectuals. Her father was a professor at the University of Santiago's School of Law, and her grandfather was a distinguished attorney with numerous artistic interests. One of her brothers was a well-known writer.

She received her elementary education at a prestigious religious institution with French ties, at which she became perfectly fluent in French. Upon completion of her secondary studies, she enrolled in the humanities program of the University of Santiago de Compostela.

After she married, and during the Spanish Civil War (1936–39), she resided on occasion in Valencia and Barcelona, and spent long periods in Bordeaux, where she studied French literature.

When the war ended, she went into exile in Mexico with her husband. At first they lived in Campeche, on the Yucatán Peninsula, where both taught at the university there. The impressions made on Concha Castroviejo by nature and the customs of the area were reflected in some of the short stories that she wrote afterwards. Finally, she moved to Mexico City, where she lived until the end of the 1940s. It was there that her only daughter was born.

Upon her return to Spain, she took up residence once again in Santiago de Compostela and began writing articles for local newspapers. In 1953, after having obtained her diploma from the School of Journalism, she moved to Madrid to join the staff of the well-known daily *Informaciones*, for which she worked until 1966, performing a variety of tasks, writing her own column, and supervising a children's supplement that enjoyed great success with younger readers.

In 1957 she published *Those Who Went Away* (Los que se fueron), her first novel. It was followed by another novel, *Eve of Hate* (Víspera

15

del odio) in 1959, which received the Elisenda de Moncada Prize in 1958 and was translated into French in 1965.

Besides her work at *Informaciones* Concha Castroviejo contributed articles of literary criticism and pieces of her short fiction to publications like *Ínsula, La Estafeta Literaria, Blanco y Negro,* and *Q.P.*

The Garden with Seven Gates (El jardín de las siete puertas), her first book of children's stories, appeared in 1961 and won the Doncel Prize the same year. This collection was translated into Slovak in 1973.

When she left *Informaciones* she wrote the delightful tale titled *Lina's Days* (Los días de Lina) with grant support from the Juan March Foundation. It came out in 1971 and has been reissued several times.

During this period Concha Castroviejo began to work at the Official Spanish News Agency. After she left it, she wrote as a literary critic for the prestigious morning paper *La Hoja del Lunes.*

She was a member of the Association Internationale des Critiques Littéraires and served for many years on the panel of the Spanish Literary Criticism Prize.

A tireless reader, Concha Castroviejo died in Madrid in 1995.

(Translated from the Spanish by RMF)

Introduction

Carolina Fernández Rodríguez

THE STORIES IN this volume were originally intended for Spanish children of the 1960s. Now, thanks to Professor Fedorchek's fine translations, English-speaking children of the twenty-first century will have the opportunity to enjoy the tales that have pleased several generations of Spaniards so far. However, it is my belief that, because of the complex relationship of these stories with the fairy-tale genre, and due also to some underlying themes that pervade the collection and relate it to the poverty-stricken Spain of the post–Civil War years (or, more generally, to any country that has known the horrors of war), the book we are now holding in our hands may be a source of pleasure for adults too.

Concha Castroviejo (Santiago de Compostela 1910–Madrid 1995) published *The Garden with Seven Gates* in 1961. This book constituted her first major foray into the field of children's literature, although it was not to be the only one. In 1971 she published a novel likewise intended for a young reading public: *Los días de Lina* (Lina's days), which tells the story of a girl's discovery of the natural world. Years before the publication of these two works, Castroviejo had earned a degree in humanities at the university of her native city of Santiago, and had also studied French literature at the University of Bordeaux. Then the Spanish Civil War (1936–39) forced her to leave her country and seek refuge in Mexico, where she resided from 1939 to 1949. Her experiences of the war and her life as an exile might be indirectly described in *The Garden with Seven Gates,* as we will see later on, but they are clearly reflected in her two other works for adults, her novels *Los que se fueron* (Those who went away, 1957) and *Víspera del odio* (Eve of hate, 1959). Besides her career as a writer of fiction, Castroviejo worked as a journalist and a literary critic.

Not being a prolific writer, though, the impact of Castroviejo on

17

Spanish literature cannot be considered as vital as the influence exerted by other mainstream writers who are better known both at the national and the international levels. However, besides other merits, her contribution to the development and improvement of Spanish children's literature is undeniable, which explains her inclusion in several literary dictionaries of Spanish, Portuguese, and Latin American writers.*

The history of children's literature in Spain is quite a recent one. Its beginnings have been traced back to the second part of the nineteenth century, with the appearance on the literary stage of one of the best writers of the period, Fernán Caballero (pseudonym of Cecilia Böhl de Faber), and the additional role played by other writers such as Julia de Asensi, Teodoro Baró, and Manuel Ossorio Bernard. Likewise, the founding of Saturnino Calleja Fernández's publishing house in 1885, which issued numerous collections of children's stories, meant a revolutionary step forward that propelled Spanish children's literature towards the twentieth century.

In the 1910s and 1920s there were further developments and a greater advancement in the maturation process of the literature intended for Spanish youth. Children's theater, for example, benefited from the mastery of Nobel Prize–winner Jacinto Benavente (1866–1954). The supplements of a number of magazines, such as *Gente Menuda* (1928–36) and *Blanco y Negro* (1928–36), also devoted their attention to it, publishing unsophisticated plays in installments by writers like Elena Fortún, Magda Donato, and Salvador Bartolozzi. At the same time certain publishing houses helped to revitalize children's literature, thereby giving rise to renewed currents in other genres. On the whole, they placed special emphasis on the children's story, but did not fail to bring theater, as we have seen, and poetry closer to their young readers.

Nonetheless, what had become a promising scene for children's literature was abruptly dismantled by the outbreak of the Spanish Civil War in 1936. Together with other consequences, this armed conflict brought about the exile of a good number of people, intellectuals and artists among them, and the inauguration of a process of ideological

---

*See, for example, Ricardo Gullón's prestigious literary dictionary, *Diccionario de Literatura Española e Hispanoamericana* (Spanish and Latin-American dictionary) (Madrid: Alianza, 1993) or the *Dictionary of the Literature of the Iberian Peninsula,* ed. Germán Bleiberg, Maureen Ihrie, and Janet Pérez (Westport, Conn.: Greenwood Press, 1993).

indoctrination aimed at those who were left behind and who had fought on the losing side. The field of children's literature did not escape this fate. Thus in the decade of the 1940s, and still in that of the 1950s, political criteria quite often prevailed over literary or aesthetic principles. Plays, poems, and stories for children were molded as subtle or even obvious ideological pamphlets that the establishment used for its own purpose. For example, the Sección Femenina (Feminine Section) and the Frente de Juventudes (Youth Front), both part of the Spanish Falangist Movement, used some of their publications, such as *Bazar* (Bazaar), *Consigna* (Slogan), and *Maravillas* (Wonders), to publish plays and tales imbued with reactionary ideas. In the postwar years, then, the integrity of the literary production aimed at children was not easily maintained, although there were some notable writers like Elizabeth Mulder, María Luz Morales, Celia Viñas, and María Luisa Gefaell who refused to indoctrinate children in the principles advocated by the dictatorial regime.

As the 1950s went by, a few things began to change in the field of children's literature. The appearance of the Lazarillo Prize (1958) and the first publications of the Doncel Publishing House, one of several specializing in children's literature, paved the way for the emergence in the 1960s of a large group of writers who were devoted to the younger sections of the reading public. Together with literary figures like Ana María Matute, Carmen Kurtz, Ángela C. Ionescu, Montserrat del Amo, and Juan A. de Laiglesia, among many others, Concha Castroviejo, the author of *The Garden with Seven Gates,* was responsible for the thematic and formal renewal of Spanish children's literature. She formed part of this generation of writers who definitely contributed to healing the wounds inflicted on this genre by the Civil War. Theirs is also the merit of making the 1960s a golden age of children's literature.

It is, therefore, in this context that we should now turn our attention to *The Garden with Seven Gates,* a collection of fourteen tales and a minidrama that Concha Castroviejo published in 1961. The book gets its name from the title of the play, which is placed at the end of the work as a dramatic culmination of some of the most important themes that recur in the stories that come before it. I should consequently start by saying a few words about those narratives that set the tone of the whole work.

The tales are of a varied nature, so there is no way that one can possibly find a single category to define them all. As a result, the reading of the collection becomes a gratifying and continually exciting experience, since one can never know what kind of story comes next.

Some of the texts resemble traditional literary fairy tales in a number of ways. For example, we find stories like "The Country That Had No Birds," "A Mermaid and a Magistrate . . . ," "Martolán, Apprentice Magus," and "Karlantán and Prince Atal's Pearls" that take place in a setting that is remote, indefinite, or simply a figment of the imagination. The time when the narrated events occur is ambiguous, too— as it is in all traditional fairy tales—in stories like "The Country That Had No Birds" and "The Pirates of *The Terrible One*." The collection abounds with third-person narrators, as well as with supernatural and fantastic elements: there are stories of a talking bird in "The Sparrow and the Moon," of a kindhearted giant who liberates a number of slaves in "Barú and the Giant," and of a persuasive sea that knows all the rules of rhetoric in "The Little Girl and the Sea." A couple of tales are also related to the fairy-tale genre in their use of two different intertextual devices: explicit reference to a specific fairy tale, in one instance, and the use of a motif already typified by folklorists, in the other. Thus, in "Barú and the Giant" one reads that "Since the days of Tom Thumb giants have been vegetarians" (p. 72), a statement that functions as an intertextual mechanism and forces the reader to pursue the connection between Castroviejo's text and the canon of literary fairy tales, as well as to fix on the differences, to which I will refer later on. In "The Weaver of Dreams," on the other hand, one cannot fail to notice that the motif of the old spinster who teaches a young girl how to use the distaff makes readers associate the story with tales of the Sleeping Beauty type. Finally, the presence of happy endings in tales like "The Country That Had No Birds," "The Sparrow and the Moon," and "The Weaver of Dreams" provides one more proof that some of the texts of *The Garden with Seven Gates* bear close resemblance to the fairy-tale genre in its most classical form.

However, other stories depart from this model. "The Year That Fell into the Sea," for instance, has an intrafictional first-person narrator, and the text, on the whole, is closer to the legend than to the fairy tale; "Martolán, Apprentice Magus," for its part, is a story that, very much in the style of myths, explains the origin of starfish; "The Conceited Buzzard," a tale full of talking animals, can be better understood as a fable; and, lastly, with its stark realism and first-person narrator, "We Have the Stars" could be considered an almost naturalistic short story.

The endings of a goodly number of the stories also contribute to the readers' disassociation of *The Garden with Seven Gates* from traditional fairy tales. In fact, the predominance of unhappy endings and, in particular, the fatal or tragic denouement of many characters' lives, is one of the factors that have led me to state that Castroviejo's collection is not precisely a book of children's literature, and that even if it may have been primarily aimed at a young reading public, it might be best comprehended in all its tragicomic dimensions by an adult audience. These examples should suffice to help us gather an idea of the pessimism that pervades some of Castroviejo's stories: "We Have the Stars" concludes with the death of a grandfather and a seemingly bleak future for his grandson; at the end of "Blas's Dream" we learn that the main character, a child called Blas, is not understood by his closest relatives; "A Mermaid and a Magistrate" finishes with a siren who epitomizes failure as both a beauty and a singer; and finally, the plots of "Matías the Half-wit" and "The Little Girl and the Sea" are resolved with the deaths of an innocent boy and a kindhearted girl, respectively.

But these unfortunate or even fatal endings are not the only elements of the negative vision of life seen in this collection. Many characters suffer deprivation, hunger, poverty, ridicule, or the effects of war. It almost seems as if Castroviejo's imagination was incapable of conceiving a world devoid of some kind of torment, as if her personal experience of the Spanish Civil War and the painful observation of the poverty-stricken Spain of the postwar years from her Mexican exile had left her virtually unable to create a perfectly happy world. In this sense, Castroviejo is very much a product of her times, the natural outcome of a period, those postwar decades in which even the heroes of some comics for children were paupers who could do little more than to dream of baked chickens. Not even people who are now in their thirties, and who therefore had not even been born at that time, have been able to forget Carpanta, the poorest and hungriest of all Spanish comic heroes.

And just as she is the product of her times in this respect, we could say that the few instances when her narrative shows little sensibility towards minority groups, she is actually resorting to the stereotypical images that filled most Spaniards' minds until well into the 1980s, when Spain, and the Spanish language in particular, began to awaken from the shame of racism and imperialism. It is to these stigmas that we should attribute the fisherman's daughter's unquestioning reference, in "The Little Girl and the Sea," to the fact that the sea brings steamships "from Asia and Africa, loaded with cinnamon, elephants, and monkeys, and little blacks dressed in yellow" (p. 78), or some of the references to the slave system that lack any kind of criticism whatsoever, as in "Karlantán and Prince Atal's Pearls," in which Prince Atal informs King Tayul and Princess Karlantán of "how the slaves brought from the islands of the South immersed themselves in the sea, with both feet held fast on a big stone that was hitched to a rope, thus to descend to the depths in which the nacre shells envelop the marvelous pearls" (p. 85).

Her spatial, cultural, and historical context should also be taken into consideration in order to account for the lack of resourceful heroines that inundate the work of many British and American writers of fairy tales and children's stories from the 1970s onwards. The impact of Second Wave feminism did not obviously begin to affect Spanish writers until the 1980s, so there is little sense in reading Castroviejo's *The Garden with Seven Gates*, published in 1961, with the aim of unveiling protofeminist characters or discovering evident attacks on patriarchal discourses. Likewise, the interest in deconstructivist practices or other literary techniques generally associated with poststructuralist and postmodern approaches to the literary fairy tale in the last decades are hard to find in Castroviejo's book.

Yet, if we pay careful attention to her work, it is not impossible to locate some instances of unorthodox elements that make it veer, if only slightly, away from what was considered conventional in the Spain of the 1960s. Subtle attacks on the status quo as a whole can be seen in "Barú and the Giant," in which we learn the story of a young boy who conceives the way in which the slave system that sustains his country's economy can be dismantled. If read in connection with the fact that Spain kept her African colonies, an important source of wealth, until the late 1960s, Barú's fictitious plan might be seen to contain some kind of subversive seed that the Spanish government of the time should have mistrusted.

Women's inferior condition in a patriarchal regime is another topic that can be occasionally glimpsed in the collection. In "The Weaver of Dreams," for example, one can see the kind of traditional upbringing that a Spanish girl was expected to have in the 1960s. It involved knowing how to make lovely lace, how to iron clothes and water plants, and other such household chores. The main character, Rogelia, is unable to learn any of those tasks. However, she is tremendously quick to learn the knack of weaving dreams, an activity which, because of its intangibility, I cannot help associating with pure artistic creativity. From this perspective, then, the story would dramatize the conflict between a woman's duty towards her family and home, and her creative will; in other words, it would figuratively deal with the dichotomy of procreation versus creation. Moreover, "The Weaver of Dreams" ends with the main character's decision to live with Gosvinda, the old woman who taught her how to weave dreams, instead of with her parents and sisters or a recently acquired husband, as many fairy-tale heroines do. But what makes the ending particularly idiosyncratic is the fact that, once Rogelia and Gosvinda have established themselves as housemates and partners in their ethereal business of dream-weaving, a census taker visits their house in order to obtain some data concerning their occupation and to note it in the tax ledger. When he hears Rogelia's answer that they are weavers of dreams, he simply states that that occupation does not exist and, clearing his throat, takes his leave. The census taker is therefore the proof that the patriarchal society Rogelia and Gosvinda live in is not yet ready to accept a woman's departure from her traditional roles, not even ready to conceive of such a deviation.

In "Karlantán and Prince Atal's Pearls" both Princess Karlantán and her wet nurse show greater common sense and intelligence than all the savants in the kingdom. However, at the end of the story Castroviejo's narrative goes beyond this slight subversion by making the narrator ironically comment on the means by which the establishment, in this case represented by the kingdom's savants, manages to verify the truth about the origin of Prince Atal's pearls through consulting the historical records. This anecdote, which could stand for all the cases in which history has been used to serve the interests of those in power, can be seen as an early literary enunciation of poststructuralist critics' defense of the "textuality of history." Thus, the narrator's critique of the official historical record, which appears in the tale as a master-narrative that cannot be fully trusted, brings Castroviejo's collection ideologically closer to the postmodern condition.

But there is, in my view, yet another text in which Castroviejo's originality as a writer of children's literature becomes evident. I am referring to the minidrama that winds up *The Garden with Seven Gates*. This play constitutes a departure from the rest of the stories in terms of literary genre, but, otherwise, it represents the culmination of a number of issues, themes, and attitudes that have been present in the book from the beginning. Where does its newness reside, then?

The final text of Castroviejo's collection dramatizes the story of two children, Félix and Adrián, who have just escaped from an asylum. Both are on their way to the sea, where they plan to win absolute freedom. But while they are looking for it, they come across an old woman called Marconia who offers them her imaginary garden, a peculiar

Eden that an artist is supposedly painting for her. Adrián, the younger child, chooses to remain with old Marconia, only to lead, we are made to suppose, a life of poverty, coldness, and hunger, while the older one, Félix, decides to continue his search. However, by the end of the drama we learn that some officers have captured him and are taking him back to the asylum. Adrián and Marconia, for their part, simply disappear from the stage, and nothing more is known about them.

As this brief summary shows, thematically speaking the play is in perfect keeping with the rest of the tales in the collection. In it we likewise encounter characters that are plagued by destitution, starvation, coldness, and lack of affection. As we also saw in some of the other stories, the characters' need to daydream and cherish illusions of a better life is brutally shattered by a cruel reality: the world Castroviejo depicts is devoid of tenderness and justice; in it there is little hope that dreams can ever come true. To emphasize this point even more, the minidrama finishes not only on a pessimistic note, but also with an open ending that leaves readers wondering what, if anything, can be done to improve one's lot in life.

The irrationality of the situation is such that the whole drama is touched by a stroke of absurdity. Even a good-hearted character like Marconia shares in this incongruity. Her conviction that an artist is about to paint her a beautiful garden where she and Adrián will be able to lead a pleasant life is one example of the illogicality of some of her remarks. Instances when she gives an answer that is totally unrelated to the question she has been asked further confirm her farcical nature. Finally, the fact that she is waiting for someone, but is unable to say just who, brings her closer to Beckett's characters in *Waiting for Godot;* they all inhabit a dehumanized world where meaning is no longer attainable. This connection between a drama for children and the theater of the absurd is one of the features that makes Castroviejo's work a special landmark in the development of children's literature in the Spanish context of the 1960s—a milestone that points out the regeneration that the field began to experiment with in that decade after the impoverished period, literarily speaking, of the post–Civil War years.

It is precisely to these years and the internal conflict that shook Spain in the 1930s that I have attributed the pessimism that pervades the whole book, but, paradoxically, they might likewise be responsible, at least to a certain extent, for the idiosyncratic elements that distinguish it from other works of fairy stories and the like. Whatever the causes, however, The *Garden with Seven* Gates remains an interesting and worthwhile incursion into the territory of Spanish children's literature of the 1960s, one that is sure to move readers to consider matters as varied as some of the issues that have been discussed in this introduction, from the desirability of keeping clear-cut distinctions between adult literature and children's literature, to the structural violence of social systems that contrive to write the death certificate of dreams and illusions of all kinds.

Oviedo, November 2002

The Garden
with Seven Gates

We Have the Stars

I WAS TIRED as I dragged my feet up the stairs. It shouldn't have worn me out to climb fifty steps, since I was only ten years old. But I was hungry. All day long I had tramped through windy streets with my grandfather.

I kept track of the steps during the climb. I knew like a book that there were ten on the first flight, eight on the second, and six farther up, until reaching the rickety flights with the broken handrail that led to the attic. Grandfather climbed slowly, already looking forward to the recount of his coins. I also knew like a book what would come afterwards.

"Andrés, my son," Grandfather would say to me when he had the piles of change set out on the stool that served as his desk, "Andrés, I still have enough left for a bottle of wine. But you have to be careful, all right? Don't let the doorman and his wife see you. Go to the tavern around the corner and have them wrap the bottle for you. If the doorman sees you with it and asks questions, tell him it's olive oil. All right, Andrés? Pay close attention to everything. When you come back, supper'll be ready for you."

Grandfather then gave me the bottle that I was to have filled at the tavern. He hid it for me inside my jacket, sent me on my way, and stood next to the open door waiting to hear my footsteps on the stairs.

This happened almost every night. Grandfather brought home his ration of wine, hiding the bottles very carefully. But when we reached our room and he counted the coins he always discovered that he had a few left over to buy more wine. He said only a little more, the amount necessary to be prepared just in case he couldn't buy any the following day.

Grandfather, the poor man, suffered a great deal on account of the wine. He suffered because of me, and that made me experience even more emotion as I ran those mysterious errands, taking precautions with which we didn't fool anyone.

When my mother, his daughter, died, Grandfather had come to the house for me, a house already stripped of furniture because my mother, a widow, had had to sell one piece after another during her illness. All that remained was the bed and some other things, and the clothes that a few neighbor women were keeping in an old trunk. Several pious ladies who had had a hand in my mother's funeral said that a drunken vagabond like my grandfather should not assume the upbringing of a little boy. They compiled information and wrote a few papers to have me taken into an institution. Grandfather had to make a solemn promise not to get drunk again. He couldn't promise that he would stop being a vagabond because his only means of support was his violin and the good will of the people who listened to him by the bar in taverns or in the corners of squares. It's what he had always done.

"I could have been an artist, Andrés," he would often say to me. "A great artist. But fortune didn't smile on me. I had little money and many needs and had to earn a living. How was I going to wait to be booked for one of those concerts that are announced at theaters? When I began to play in the street everybody looked down on me."

Grandfather had studied at the Conservatory for many years. People always reproached him for the way in which he began to go downhill because of the wine. I knew because the neighbor women used to stop to ask me questions, and the lady who lived on the second floor complained, in front of me, about the bad education that I was receiving. She was a lady who usually gave me good advice, and she told me that Grandfather had let his wife die in neglect and in poverty.

"It's not true, Andrés," Grandfather explained to me. "I'll grant that the poor thing had no comforts, but I took care of her all the time. I spent entire afternoons entertaining her with my violin. It was what she liked best. Listening to me play. Hour after hour, even if got tired, I played for her during her illness. And she was content."

Once when my grandfather had brought me to his room in the attic, the women who had wanted to send me to the institution took it upon themselves to watch over me. Of course it's true that entire months passed without their remembering me, but sometimes they inquired into whether I was attending school and whether my grandfather came home drunk at night. The doorman's wife liked to get on well with prominent people and regarded us with hostility. Grandfather and I shook in our boots in her presence, and in that of her husband, who was a watchman at the jail and spent his afternoons sitting in their nook at the entrance so that his wife could go out. The two of them terrified us. As he thought about their scrutiny Grandfather almost did not dare to drink in the taverns where he was frequently offered a glass.

"Wine is good, Andrés," he would say to me. "Good for old men like me. But if they find out that I'm drinking, they'll take you to the institution. You don't want to go to the institution, do you, Andrés?"

No. I did not want to go to the institution. I was happy with our life, with our hunger, with our attic, with Grandfather's violin, and with that hand of his, big and rough, that squeezed mine to keep me at his side when we were out in the street.

Whenever he fell into the temptation of drinking a few glasses, Grandfather entered the hallway slowly, holding onto my arm, more respectful and polite than ever. Before entering, each night, he positioned the violin in such a way that it covered the bottle of wine that he carried in his pocket.

"I don't know why they think it's bad, Andrés," he said to me. "I just don't know. Wine is a gift from God. God put it in the world for us. Not for you, no; you're a little boy. But I'm an old man. Wine warms my bones. I don't know why they think it's bad."

Each night, when I returned from running that errand for him, Grandfather closed the door, sat down in a big old straw chair alongside his stool, and breathed with satisfaction. Afterwards he took the coins left on top of the stool and put them in a tin can. He didn't want us to be taken by surprise, unable to pay the rent at the end of the month. Grandfather knew that we were undesirables in that building of affluent, orderly tenants. He didn't dare to play the violin inside the room for fear that some neighbor might protest. Both of us quaked at the thought of eviction, the result of which would surely be that I would end up at the institution.

THAT NIGHT I came back sad as well as tired. It was January 6th, the feast of The Three Kings.* My grandfather had gone to play in a district that we did not frequent. Children were walking along the streets with their new toys and I thought that never, in many years, had I had a toy. I envied the pastry rolls that I saw in show windows, the bags of candy, and the good, comfortable clothes.

---

* The traditional day in Spain for giving Christmas gifts. *Trans.*

When we entered our attic I glanced around. My grandfather had lit, as he usually did, a candle in order to climb the last dark flights, and by the light of the flame, in a kind of chiaroscuro, our room didn't strike me as completely desolate. But by the light of the dirty electric bulb hanging from the ceiling I made out, like something new, the big, ramshackle bed, the wobbly table on which were two earthenware casserole dishes and several plates, the stool, Grandfather's chair, the rusty iron washstand, and the fireplace of broken stones, which was greasy from smoke and fat, where we made a fire and cooked with the grill and the pots on the days that we ate hot food. I felt so sad that I turned to Grandfather and exclaimed:

"We don't have anything!"

Grandfather then went over to the window and opened it to the night.

"Look," he said to me. "We have the stars."

I looked outside. In the dry night, under the black sky, thousands of stars shone above us.

"We have the stars," Grandfather repeated. "All of God's stars."

And because he saw the joy of discovery in my eyes he added:

"*We* have them. God put them there for us. The people who walk the streets don't raise their heads to see them. The people who live in nice homes, with curtains on the windows, don't look at them either. Only from our attic do you see them shine like this. They're ours."

My grandfather turned to me again. He had played the violin all day long on bitterly cold streets and his fingers were swollen. He was tired and numb. But, since we had brought back an ample amount of wine and he could feed me a good supper, he was also content. He put his hand on my head and smiled.

"God gave them to me," he said, gazing at the stars, "and now I'm giving them to you."

Sitting by the fire, I ate bread and the sausages that we grilled, and then got into bed. Grandfather opened the window again and took the violin from its case. Something he never did. But that was a solemn night. Very softly he began to play Schubert's sonata, for me, and in honor of the stars that he had given me as a gift.

THAT WAS A harsh winter. And on the heels of winter came the sunny months during which Grandfather played at get-togethers in the country. On pilgrimages people gave us food from what they carried in their baskets and glasses of good wine for Grandfather. Then fall arrived and another and more harsh winter.

I had been living with Grandfather for five years. He made me attend school so that he would not be accused of neglect, but I frequently played hooky and never finished the subjects. I preferred to accompany him, to listen to him talk or play his violin. It seemed to me that he played like the angels. Some people said that he no longer had agility in his fingers, that he confused notes and that his violin was out of tune. But I didn't believe them.

So for five years I had been living a life of poverty and happiness when Grandfather took sick. The winter was raw and his wool vest was ragged. We had rummaged through my mother's trunk. Until then Grandfather had never wanted to open it.

"It's for you, Andrés; it's your inheritance."

But since it was so cold we went through it to look for warm clothes. We removed a few undershirts and put another blanket on the bed.

Despite everything Grandfather began to cough and one day could not get up. I stayed at his side. I covered him well and lit a fire in the fireplace to make soup for him. When I went to the tavern the following day to buy him his wine the tavernkeeper said to me:

"Here. Take this to him. It'll revive him."

And he gave me a white bottle filled with brandy.

Grandfather was very grateful for it. He sat up in bed, poured brandy in a glass, and drank a few swallows.

"This is good stuff, Andrés, very good. I can go out tomorrow for sure."

But he couldn't. He was worse.

I didn't know what needed to be done. I went in search of the doctor from the street and spent the savings in the tin can to buy the medicines that he prescribed. I couldn't pay the doctor, and the medicines didn't help Grandfather at all, because he began to breathe with difficulty and could not swallow them.

The woman who came every morning to clean the stairs, and who was a good woman, as poor as we were, called the priest from our parish. Grandfather could no longer talk. When the priest left, he said to me:

"If you see that he stops breathing, don't be frightened, but notify the doorman's wife at once."

That night Grandfather breathed his last. I thought that if I notified the doorman and his wife, they would immediately send some men who would take Grandfather away from our attic. I thought that Grandfather would have wanted to stay a few hours more with his violin and me at his side. I closed the door. I covered the bed with a bedspread that I took from my mother's trunk; I stretched out Grandfather's body, positioned his head on the pillow, and washed his face with a wet rag. Afterwards I placed his violin at the foot of the bed and sat down next to the headboard. I was hungry, sleepy, and cold, but that wasn't what mattered to me.

My eyes burned from so much crying. Most of all, though, I felt miserable because I couldn't offer anything to Grandfather. He was dead, and I had neither flowers nor candles for him. I didn't even have a casket in which to lay him out before he was lowered into the ground. That idea of the casket tormented me because I thought it was the final humiliation, that poor Grandfather should have to be carried from his room wrapped in a sheet, in full view of everybody.

Through the window there came a white brightness as strong as the yellow brightness from our dirty electric bulb. It had snowed during the day, and now, in the cloudless, mist-free sky and cold air, the stars shone. The window was in the wall beside the headboard of the bed, and the stellar light did not illuminate Grandfather's face.

I climbed up on the stool where he had counted his change so many times and pulled the cord that secured the wood trapdoor on the roof. A big square covered with glass opened up in the midst of the tiles. Through the square, above Grandfather's head, all the stars shone in the black sky, just as they did the night that he gave them to me.

I had nothing else to offer him, and it seemed to me that Grandfather would have liked being surrounded by the light of the stars when he could no longer see them.

Blas's Dream

ONE NIGHT BLAS succeeded in doing what no child had ever done: he succeeded in seeing Sleep.

Blas knew that it was difficult. When daylight woke him each morning he wanted to remember how he had fallen asleep, and he didn't remember anything. Sleep had entered and overcome him before he could note its presence. That's Sleep's secret: to put children to sleep without the children seeing it. But Blas decided to surprise it and stayed alert, in the darkness, with his eyes open.

That's how he managed to see Sleep.

Children's Sleep is the color of honey. It's not like the one that grown-ups have, which gets lost and darkens in a mass of branches until becoming black. Children's Sleep is like thick, golden honey, with neither shape nor dimensions. It always comes and it never fails. But no one knows where it walks, nor how it enters, nor when it leaves . . .

Blas simply became aware that it was there and said to it:

"Take me with you to see how children throughout the world fall asleep."

And Sleep took him along.

Sleep neither rests nor stops. It's always alert; it's everywhere. It puts children to sleep at night; it puts them to sleep in the afternoon at nap time; it puts them to sleep when they cry and when they're sick. And if a child's mother dies, Sleep hurries and envelops him in its golden cloak and paints him a horizon of smiles. Sleep has no days off and no hours of repose. Sleep goes to every country and to every town. It approaches the cradles that are on Earth and the cradles that rock to and fro on the boats that cross the seas.

Blas sped through the air with Sleep and saw how it would go in—only for an instant—to check on sleeping children. Afterwards it would come out and take Blas farther and farther away. And unexpectedly Sleep flew so high that it seemed to Blas that Earth was very distant and had the shape of a ball.

This occurred when they were flying over the Himalayas. They encountered the other Sleep there—the Sleep of grown-ups. It's a tired and old Sleep who has bitter wings and who many nights spreads a dark red cape that imprisons anxieties and fears without letting them escape. It's the deep and slow Sleep, the one that sometimes forgets its obligations and doesn't put to sleep people who are very tired or very sad.

Children's Sleep explained to Blas:

"A child becomes a grown-up, a real grown-up, when I leave him, when we make the switch and I turn him over to my companion, the other Sleep that you saw just now. In order for me to be able to notify him, we meet every day."

"And who notifies you, Sleep?"

"The angels notify me. There's an angel who tells me where children are born each day."

Sleep kept on flying and extended its honey-colored cape over all the beds where children lay. Blas noticed that once again they were up very high, and it seemed to him that Earth was farther and farther below, small and round, spinning like a top. He shuddered and sought refuge in Sleep's wings.

IT BEGAN TO get light. Blas saw that they were flying over a meadow and that Earth was level and still as when he walked on it. Sleep said:

"I'm going to show you my mountain pass."

Sleep has a cool, serene pass that is unlike any other place on Earth. When there are wars or epidemics, or many misfortunes occur, mothers stay up at night to watch for Sleep's arrival and say to it:

"Take the children and keep them safe until Death goes away."

And Sleep takes the children to the magic pass. The children fall asleep, and the slopes fill with the races of white hares and the air with the flights of blue- and yellow-winged dragonflies.

If the war ends and the plague disappears, the mothers go to the pass.

"Sleep," say the Japanese mothers, "give us our children, because the almond trees are flowering again."

"We have tea and rice now," say the mothers from China. "The evil spirits have gone away. We can take them back, Sleep."

"Give them to us, there's no more war," sigh the mothers from Europe.

The children go, and the pass becomes quiet.

"YOU'VE SEEN EVERYTHING now," Sleep said to Blas. "But you'll never see me again."

"You won't take me to your pass any more?"

"I'll take you, for the last time, before I have to notify the grown-ups' Sleep for you."

By the light of dawn Sleep was flying toward Blas's bed, in more and more of a hurry.

"Where are you going now?" Blas said.

"I'm going to America. Night is falling there, and it's their custom to put children to bed very early. I can't be delayed."

Sleep encircled Blas with its wings and left him asleep in his bed, in a world of white hares and yellow butterflies.

"BLAS, BLAS!" his older brother shouted. "You'll be late to school again. I'm leaving."

"What a lazy boy!" lamented the father.

"How is it possible for you to sleep so long, Blas?" asked his mother when she went into his room to draw back the curtains.

"I didn't close my eyes," said Blas. "I waited for Sleep and it took me along. It was a marvelous journey."

But no one understood what he was saying.

The Country That Had No Birds

THIS IS THE story of how the terrible warriors of the land of Kor stopped waging wars and decided to live in peace.

The warriors of Kor were gigantic men, so strong that their arms never flagged from brandishing a lance, so strong that they could ride on horseback for days on end without becoming fatigued. The warriors of Kor had never been defeated.

In that country everybody lived for war. The meadows lost their flowers from being trampled by horses' hooves. The men who did not engage in combat forged lances and swords, and little boys trained with the toughest exercises in order to become warriors as good as their fathers. Nobody tilled the land. Nobody plowed, nobody sowed, nobody irrigated. Each spring, summer, fall, and winter the warriors carried out their raids on neighboring countries and brought back a plentiful booty with everything necessary—they brought the wheat of abundant harvests, textiles, cattle, and gold. With all this the fields no longer produced anything and the slate roads that crisscrossed the country sparkled on contact with hooves and echoed with the clashing of lances.

When they had their booty assured, the warriors prepared forays to distant kingdoms so that they might afterwards return with carts laden with trophies and the glory of victory. The king retained on salary twelve poets who sang of the feats and courage of the warriors of Kor. So well did they know their craft that, when they composed an epic poem to be read at the great banquets with which victories were celebrated in the stone halls of the castle, the king measured the parchments with a hazel stick. If the poem was not long enough, he would say to them:

"You have to add another length of verses."

And the poets set to composing stanzas until completing the number desired by the king.

All year long they wrote with quills on rolls of parchment in order to be prepared with songs at any given moment. That was because in the land of Kor the warriors covered many miles and overpowered countries with more speed than the poets could compose stanzas. And thus, if in winter the warriors rested while waiting for the snow to melt, the poets would begin to write a poem that extolled the spring campaign.

ONE DAY THE king, riding on horseback through the woods that surrounded the castle, observed the strange silence that reigned there. He then gathered together the nobles and poets in the great hall of arms and asked:

"Why is there so much silence in our fields?"

No one could give him an answer. Finally a minstrel much despised by the poets said:

"Sire, in the country of Kor there no longer are birds."

"There no longer are birds? And no one has informed me of this occurrence?"

The warriors confessed their ignorance and the poets showed surprise on their faces.

"What kind of poets do we have in Kor?" exclaimed the king. "They don't know when springtime arrives, nor do they realize that not a single bird sings in our woods."

The poets, highly offended, stated that they didn't have the time to concern themselves with things of so little importance.

"Fine," said the king. "You're neither poets nor persons of any consequence. You may leave us."

The poets collected their quills, their rolls of parchment, and the hazel stick with which they measured the length of a poem, and departed to offer their services to sovereigns who were getting ready to celebrate weddings or wished to sing the glories of their ancestors.

But the warriors of Kor were saddened. They liked birds. They remembered the good days when the woods were alive with warbles and the air rent with swift, dark or brilliant wings.

Thus it was that all the inhabitants of Kor began to think of a way to get the birds to return to their fields.

"They left," said an old man, "because they couldn't find anything to eat—there's no wheat, no barley, no fruit, no grass. The land isn't tilled. We bring in everything from other kingdoms and the birds left."

The king ordered the capture of a cuckoo, which is a very gossipy bird. He had all the roads in the country covered with grains of wheat and then ordered the release of the cuckoo, which flew off to give the news to his companions. From the North and the South, from the East and the West, birds began to arrive in flocks and blanketed the plain, eating and singing, satisfied with their lot.

When the flagstones and cracks were cleaned of grain, the birds took flight, surveying the countryside, and left once again.

"It's going to be necessary to till the land," the old man repeated.

And the king ordered all the nobles to have the soldiers till their lands.

So much did they plow, sow, irrigate, and prune that the best harvests that year were gathered in the country of Kor. When spring arrived the birds turned up in the woods, in the fields, and in the orchards. They became so trustful and felt so familiar that it is said that when the king was getting ready to taste the first cherries, a blackbird alighted on his shoulder and began to peck at them with no respect for the royal personage.

The woods once more filled with warbles and nests, and the air with flights.

This gladdened the inhabitants of Kor. All the warriors were content.

At that time neither foreign exchange nor freezers had been invented, and nobody wanted to harvest more than what they needed. Since they harvested so much in Kor, the king and the warriors agreed not to go off in search of booty and stayed home to enjoy the beauty of the fields.

Then the forgers of arms said to the king:

"What will be done with all the leftover lances and swords?"

The king organized a great joust on the esplanade of the castle. Five hundred knights engaged in combat by turns for eight days and broke more than three thousand lances against the armor of their opponents.

Afterwards the blacksmiths melted down the pieces and forged metal fences for the tilled land.

The king kept an armed guard in reserve to defend the country and divided the land among the soldiers. The nobles returned to their castles. They liked peace so much and obtained such beautiful harvests that for many years it did not occur to them to undertake a single raid. And all the kingdoms that surrounded the fearsome country of Kor could live in peace.

This is how the birds, so scorned by twelve poets, changed the lives of the invincible warriors.

The Sparrow and the Moon

THE MOON HAS become very small, split in half, and thin, like a slice of lemon in syrup. But it's still conceited and pleased with itself, and very willingly tells the person who asks it why it was split in half.

However, the one who knows this story from the beginning, in great detail, is the sparrow, the only sparrow that stayed in the meadow that winter of so many snowfalls. The poor sparrow couldn't find a single bread crumb or a single grain of wheat in the white mantle that covered the ground, and it was so cold that it didn't know if it was going to die from the cold or from hunger. It was thinking of its fate and very sad when it saw, like a spot on the ice, Señora Brunilda, who lived in the garden cottage with her children.

Señora Brunilda was very compassionate. She opened the window so that the sparrow could fly in to get warm, and gave it, all crumbled up, a piece of biscuit that Patricia had left on her plate. The sparrow decided to accept such good hospitality until spring and only went out each morning for a flight so as not to get out of the habit. During the rest of the day it played with the three children, and at night it chirped on Patricia's bed to help her fall asleep. It was a well-mannered sparrow, and took care not to soil the rug in the dining room, nor the big sparkling glass fruit bowl, with pieces of wax fruit in it, that Señora Brunilda set in the center of the table as a decoration. Nor did it soil the lamps or the polished pots and pans hanging in the kitchen. The mother was very content and the children became good friends with the sparrow.

The father, who was a very serious man, said from time to time: "Where's the sparrow? It must go and see if spring is coming."

The sparrow obeyed and flew as far as the reed beds that bordered the river. When it returned it would apprise the children's father of what it had seen:

"The water's not flowing yet and the trees have no buds."

41

The owner of the house would then snort under his muffler and go to read the newspaper by the stove. The mother headed for the kitchen to prepare more syrup in case the children caught cold again.

But one day spring arrived. The sparrow came across it all of a sudden when it set out on its morning flight and, as always happens to sparrows, spring went to its head. It no longer remembered to return to the cottage. That night Patricia couldn't fall asleep, because the sparrow wasn't there to chirp on her bed, and the other children didn't want to turn in without knowing if the sparrow would come back or if spring had carried it off forever.

The sparrow spent a very happy month. With each passing day the sun was warmer and warmer and the trees offered better and better branches. The birds arrived in flocks, from the North and from the South, and they all greeted one another with the utmost courtesy. The swallows, very serious in their formal dress, were the ones that put on the most airs.

At the cottage they continued to miss the sparrow, and the father would say:

"How ill-mannered! It hasn't even come to thank us."

But the truth is that, when it had greeted all its companions and they had the branches evenly divided, the sparrow showed up and flew into the cottage to find out how the family was. It met a very displeased Señora Brunilda.

"The children can't sleep," she explained. "At first we blamed you, Sparrow, but now we know why it is: the Moon has grown a lot and gives off more and more light. All night long it's reflected in the window of the children's room and doesn't let them rest."

"Goodness gracious," exclaimed the sparrow, "what an inconsiderate moon! It's necessary to be a little more prudent and not penetrate people's houses like that."

When it returned to its branch, the sparrow related to the other sparrows what was occurring, and they all began to criticize the Moon. A swallow that happened to be flying by there said:

"Those parents need to be told to buy curtains."

But the sparrows, who are well-mannered, understood that such a thing would be an impertinence.

The sparrow that was the children's friend could not sleep all night thinking about the fact that the children were not sleeping, and the following day, early in the morning, it appeared at the cottage.

"Hang a piece of biscuit around my neck," it said to Señora Brunilda, "because I'm going to be flying to the Moon to tell it what's happening."

And, very determined, the sparrow headed for the Moon. It had to fly so much that its wings hurt, and its neck swelled from fatigue. It flew all day long, and when night came it would alight on the stars that it encountered along the way. Little by little the entire sky was being covered with stars and, hopping from one to another, it arrived at the Moon, perched on the highest rim so that the children could see it from the window, and explained what was happening.

"What do you want me to do?" answered the Moon. "I'm so beautiful and so bright that my light goes everywhere."

"And can't you go and position yourself in another spot where you'll be hidden between big, unknown mountains?"

"What would wayfarers do at night? What would ships do? And what would be said by the fish that turn silver, thanks to me?"

The sparrow began to feel sad and an idea occurred to the Moon:

"I have a mind to travel. If you're capable of splitting me in half with your bill, I'll divide my beauty into two skies and my light won't frighten any child."

So the sparrow, setting aside the remainder of the biscuit that it had been nibbling as it hopped from star to star, began to peck the big ball that was the Moon as stonecutters do stone. The Moon, so plump and so showy, was soft as cream cheese, and before the Sun came up the sparrow had it split in two. Afterwards it took the bigger part of the Moon in its bill and hung it beneath a cloud that was passing by very quickly on its way to carry rain to the desert.

When it saw that slice of orange instead of the vain ball that boasted of light, the sparrow bowed very politely and very quickly headed back to Earth. The journey seemed more relaxed, and a cloud that was going to settle over the mountain near the cottage very willingly carried the sparrow along in its cotton puffs.

On arriving at the cottage, it met Señora Brunilda, who was very busy sewing .

"I'm coming from the Moon," said the sparrow.

"You must be very tired," Señora Brunilda responded. "Rest wherever you like. In the kitchen cupboard, which is open, you'll find cookies. The children won't be long. I'm finishing the curtains that I'm sewing for the window of their room, and this way they'll be able to sleep peacefully tonight. They're lovely curtains that I bought from the salesman at the fair."

"I've split the Moon in two," said the sparrow. "It's light will no longer be able to bother them. They'll sleep very comfortably."

The children's father, who was a very serious man and who paid more attention to books than to what the sparrow said, arrived home from his office and explained to Señora Brunilda:

"The Moon has entered its last quarter. Even if you don't finish the curtains, the children will be able to sleep."

And the children, who were coming in from school, began to shout with joy.

"We're going to sleep happy," they said. "The sparrow has come back home."

A Mermaid and a Magistrate, 500 Neighbors, and a Singing Blackbird

NO CHILD TODAY, or twenty years ago, or a hundred, has ever seen Blonda the mermaid. The mermaid went away a long, long time ago. But before that she lived in Spain, and the entertainment for all the children on Sunday afternoons was to go to hear her sing.

The mermaid lived in a lagoon that was in Pico Sacro, a lagoon that afterwards dried up—nobody knows why, just as nobody knows where the big hole leads, the big hole at the top of the mountain. Only the moles, who have their tunnels there, and the foxes, who fashioned a big, cool storehouse to keep the chickens that they steal, are perfectly familiar with the mysterious underground passage.

But this was many centuries ago, and back then there was a very beautiful, very clean lagoon in Pico Sacro that was surrounded by trees and had banks covered with plants that flourished every spring. The mermaid lived there. No one could say when she arrived. Everybody, even elderly people, remembered her always being there, because mermaids neither age nor lose their beauty. They live for many years and when they're a century old they're as pretty as ever. For that reason they become very conceited and very haughty, and look down on everyone.

Blonda the mermaid had taken possession of the lagoon. When the weather was very bad she submerged and swam to the cave that she had on the bottom, where she was attended with great care by two turtles that served as maids. If the bad weather lasted a long time one of the turtles summoned the old frog, which descended to the cave to tell the mermaid all the animals' and people's gossip.

As soon as the sun shone the mermaid would come out and circle the lagoon, gracefully swinging her shoulders and swaying her hips.

"Let no one step on the banks," she would caution. "Let no one get entangled in my hair."

The mermaid had very long, shiny hair, and since she had been born in one of the North countries, on the coasts of the Baltic Sea, it was yellow like gold and glittered in the sunlight. So when spring came and gorse plants bloomed with yellow flowers, Blonda the mermaid liked to spread her hair over them so that everybody would find it more beautiful and more golden than the flowers themselves. The gorse plants felt very annoyed by so much presumption on the mermaid's part, but the poor gorse are humble, kindhearted plants, for which reason they hid their thorns so as not to ensnare the beautiful head of hair and allowed the weight of it to crumple the flowers on their stems.

Naturally, Blonda the mermaid liked to sing. All mermaids have to sing, it's their obligation, because that's why they're mermaids. But she was so conceited that she sang all day long, just to see how people admired her. She sang from sunrise till sunset, and during full moons, when, as everybody knows, birds do not sleep, lizards come out to take moonbaths, and bats, blinded, hang from trees with branches over the water. The mermaid, puffed up with self-satisfaction because of the amazement that she provoked, was capable of singing all night. No bird dared to object and even owls kept quiet, because it was well known that the mermaid had a nasty temper.

When the weather was good, people came from great distances to see her, not because they liked how she sang, but because they found her to be so extraordinary that they didn't want to miss the sight. They were right to do so, because in those centuries mermaids were beginning to be in short supply and it wasn't likely that a lagoon would have a permanent one. People from all over that area felt as much curiosity as we would feel if we saw that a mermaid was suddenly put in the pond of a park. Besides, in those days there were so few amusements that the chief one was the mermaid of Pico Sacro. That's why she was so conceited and so pompous.

Well, with all this, one beautiful spring the mermaid became more pleased and more haughty than ever after having obtained permission from the magistrate to found a school for singing.

"Have signs posted all around and inform everyone," she said to the villagers. "Clean up the countryside and get the roads ready, because important people from every country will come when they find out that I'm deigning to give lessons with my beautiful voice."

She was bedecked and bejeweled, covered with necklaces of precious conchs brought back to her by trout after their journeys, conchs that the turtles had to string painstakingly. Her hair had grown so much that when she swam it spread like a golden tail, overlaying the lagoon.

The mermaid felt happy.

But it was precisely that spring when a pilgrim passed by there, an old and poorly dressed man who had a bird perched on his shoulder.

The pilgrim sat down at the edge of the lagoon. He took off his sandals ,and got ready to try the water and soak his feet, which were bloody after a long journey.

"Ugh!" exclaimed the mermaid. "How dare you! To come and muddy the water for me like this!"

But the pilgrim pretended not to understand and began to gather twigs to light a fire and roast potatoes that he carried in his pouch.

"What impertinence!" said the mermaid. "Everybody has respected my domain until now. I'm going to report this. Such beautiful spots weren't made for ragged beggars."

Since it was the midday hour when all the neighbors were eating in their homes, only a little girl who was leading two cows heard the mermaid's shouts. The pilgrim continued to ignore her protests; when he finished roasting his potatoes and eating them, he stretched out on the grass, and the bird—a poor, dark, ugly bird—flew up to a branch and began to sing.

So well did it sing, and in such a marvelous way, that on receiving the notes the air seemed to change into diamonds and gold, full of clean, clear sounds that trailed off in the distant mountains.

People began to congregate, astonished, and the mermaid saw red. So cross, so angry did she get that, with a great dive, she submerged in the lagoon and descended to the bottom to quarrel with the turtles, who weren't to blame for anything.

The mermaid remained hidden until the next day, thinking, with considerable satisfaction, that everybody would notice her absence and that the magistrate would have ordered two forest rangers to expel the pilgrim who had invaded her domain, as well as the bird that had dared to sing inside the confines of the land intended to display her voice to the world.

But when she surfaced, she was greatly surprised. The bird continued to sing and people blanketed the meadow to hear it. The important neighbors had come, and even the forest rangers with their bandoleers were there, openmouthed.

"Now, that's really singing," were the first words that Blonda heard. "Not the squeaks that come from the mermaid."

And she submerged once more, but never to come out again. She headed for the dark tunnel that joined the lagoon with the river, and since she found no one to pay attention to her on reaching it, she followed the current to the sea. She believed that she would create a lot of excitement there, but people were so taken up with defending their coasts against pirates and sailors who brought such marvelous news of their travels that nobody thought it was extraordinary to see the mermaid who so conceitedly made her presence known opposite the beach.

"I'll begin to sing," said the mermaid, "and they'll come immediately to admire me."

And she began to sing. But it turned out that, as a result of her rage and the cold, she had gone hoarse and the waves drowned the sound of her voice.

Since at that time there were no pharmacies and only a few men in pointed caps laboriously prepared unguents, the poor mermaid couldn't buy pills for her throat, and, because of her anger, she became more and more hoarse. She then latched onto the keel of a fishermen's boat that was leaving for distant fishing grounds, coasts in the North.

For many years nobody heard anything about her. But it happened one time—which is how everything happens in stories—that twelve sailors arrived at the Baltic Sea to search for ambergris so that glovers could saturate ladies' gloves with its scent, which was the fashion back then, and they heard the mermaid singing songs of Pico Sacro and another one that they knew. The poor mermaid was very hoarse and sang very badly. She lived on the Isle of Failed Mermaids, where refuge is sought by all the mermaids who can no longer boast of having a voice, and they continue to reside there for many years, criticizing one another and speaking ill of the countries from which they have come.

Since mermaids live for many centuries, some still survive, and from time to time an American impresario visits the isle to see whether the mermaids can serve to shout over the radio.

But poor Blonda the mermaid is no good even for that.

Matías the Half-wit

"THE MOON'S in the sky," the children would say to the Half-wit.

But the Half-wit didn't believe them.

"The Moon," he explained to them, "is at the bottom of the water. It's in the deep well and in the pond, and sometimes it flows in the river, changing its appearance with the current."

Hearing him say it so often, the children had begun to believe the Half-wit. His name was Matías. Nobody in the town paid attention to him and only the children stopped to listen to him. When night fell, Matías sat down at the edge of the pond, waiting for the Moon to appear at the bottom of the water.

"Look, the Moon's in the sky already, Matías," the children would shout at him.

The Moon—big, round, covered with dust, and adorned with precious jewels, or the half-moon, slim and graceful—rose above the rim of the mountains. Matías would gaze at it for a moment.

"No," he would respond. "It's not in the sky. The thing is that it comes underwater from the river and is reflected. It'll reach the pond in a little while."

And when the Moon reached its zenith, it plunged into the water and quivered on the bottom.

"Here it is," Matías would say. "It's here now."

"Forget the Moon, Matías," passersby advised him. "For try as you may, you're not going to catch it."

The Half-wit's dream was to catch the full moon. He wanted to catch it and hold it down on the slimy bottom of the pond, from which it would no longer be able to budge. He wanted to keep it there, day and night, and tell people that the Moon belonged to him, to Matías.

On the nights when there was a full moon the Half-wit waited very anxiously for the Moon to appear on the pond. He then waded into the water, advancing little by little. At his passage the water would

49

begin to move in waves and he would stop, fearful that the Moon might become frightened, and stand still for awhile in order to fool it. When the water reached his waist and the slime on the bottom stirred around, the entire pond turned muddy and dark. Matías would stand still once again until the water cleared and the moon once again appeared on the bottom. Then he would dive in and emerge crestfallen, empty-handed.

Matías had no family, and it didn't matter to anyone that he got himself wet and that he came back to town stiff with cold on clear winter nights, when the Moon shone more insolently and contentedly over the frozen countryside. Matías was given, out of pity, a room in a hayloft. The children, by turns, took him food.

The schoolchildren had divided into two groups: the smart ones and the hopeful ones. The smart children knew full well that the Moon is a satellite of Earth and revolves around it. They also knew that it had no light of its own. And they knew that only its reflection is seen in the water. These children regarded Matías with compassion and thought, like all the sensible people in the town, that the mayor should have had him locked up so that he wouldn't dive into the water after the Moon, mistaking it for a fish. The hopeful children had to learn the same things in school, but did not altogether believe them. Filled with emotion, they waited for the day when Matías would emerge from the water with the Moon, heavy with glitter and glory, in the palms of his hands.

"Ask the Three Kings for the Moon," they would say to him.

But Matías thought it was more beautiful to surprise the Moon and bring it out, all wet, from the bottom of the pond, where no one believed it was. And the children understood that he was right.

"When Matías brings the Moon out," they asked, "where will he put it?"

And they themselves answered:

"He'll put it in the square in front of the church . . ."

"He'll hang it on the tower . . ."

"No," said the more knowledgeable ones. "He'll leave it in the water, securely tied so that it'll always be there. And the pond will belong to Matías."

When the schoolteacher overheard these conversations of the children, first he scolded them, and then he wrote a letter to their parents complaining that the children were not applying his scientific teachings.

One day a poet who passed by the pond said to Matías:

"Where you can catch the Moon is in the sea. In the sea there are many boats and many fishes, and the Moon doesn't suspect that you're going to catch it. It'll think you're going to look for a silver mullet or a black squid; it'll think you're looking for shells that shine on the bottom of the sand; it'll think you want the soft, green algae that quiver in the waves. The Moon in the sea is trusting and spreads its brilliant tail, its brilliant and long tail, where it puts its jewels in order to wash them."

And Matías headed for the sea. He went as far as the beach, waited for the night of the full moon, and waded into the sea after it.

TWO DAYS LATER a few fishermen found Matías's body in the water. They brought it to land and people said:

"It's the Half-wit from Samar de la Alberca."

And in Samar de la Alberca they said:

"Look how Matías wound up with that mania for the Moon. It would've been better if they had locked him up."

A couple of very serious gentlemen came to investigate what had happened. The court recorder listened to the statements of the fishermen and the townspeople and wrote everything down on big sheets of untrimmed paper; the medical examiner said that Matías had drowned; and the judge declared that no one was at fault and that, as there was no more to be done, he could be buried.

The hopeful children broke their piggy banks and collected money to buy Matías a casket lined with white cloth, white being the color of the full moon at the bottom of the pond.

The town carpenter said to the children:

"The casket has to be lined in black."

But the children went to see the parish priest, and the parish priest gave permission for the carpenter to line Matías's casket in white. Afterwards the children went in search of white flowers to cover the casket and then, very sad, set out for the cemetery.

"I believe," said the smallest child, "that Matías stayed with the Moon at the bottom of the sea."

The Year That Fell into the Sea

CONCORDIO CHU PEC the Indian told me how a foolish Old Year sank to the bottom of the sea.

Concordio the Indian was, one January 31st at five o'clock in the afternoon, sitting on a rock on his heels, with his palm-leaf hat pushed back and his possessions in front of him. The possessions were: a horn-handle knife, a leather tobacco pouch, a linen napkin in which were wrapped some dried spicy meat and a stack of maize pancakes, a jug of pulque, and a cone-shaped net with a long wood handle. Concordio the Indian was going to shove off—with his father, Epifanio Hi Gutiérrez the Indian, in the boat that belonged to both of them— to go fishing. He had been waiting for dusk since three o'clock in the afternoon. At that hour he had left his hut, in which were to be found the rest of his possessions: his wife, his son, a skillet, a pot, and four wooden spoons, plus two hammocks and two stools. He also owned a rooster (the no-good fowl was growing into a sickly specimen), and if he had a good catch of fish, Concordio the Indian would be able to fulfill his dream of buying a piglet to fatten it.

Surely Concordio the Indian thought about all this during his long wait. He seemed neither bored not tired. He continued to squat on his bare feet, watching the cove—indifferent, motionless, his hands between his knees, perhaps sad, perhaps happy, perhaps neither sad nor happy, meek before his destiny and before the world that surrounded him.

I was going from the town to the beach when I saw him. I approached and said:

"Good afternoon."

He responded:

"Good afternoon."

I knew Concordio the Indian from having seen him go around to houses to sell live fish in the early morning hours of the days of his catches.

52

"Is the canoe going out today?" I asked.

"Why, yes, it is," he answered, "right now. As soon as night falls. I've been waiting for my father since three o'clock."

In another two hours the rapid twilight of the tropics would descend on us. The Indian wasn't joking. There he sat, calm and serious. I intended to allow him to enjoy the time that he had left to meditate, but it gave me pleasure to talk with him—when it was possible to make him talk. I found a spot on the rock alongside him, also watching for the canoe that Epifanio Hi Gutiérrez was going to paddle to the beach as soon as night fell.

"Has there been good fishing these days?" I asked the Indian.

"Well, with the waters stirred by north winds there are no fish in them."

"And where do they go?" I asked again.

"Well, who knows . . . "

At that point I didn't know what to say to him. So I just stayed there sharing in the Indian's impassiveness, drowsy in the sun, letting time pass—who knows why—without continuing on my way.

Then, after a long while, of his own accord Concordio the Indian began to tell me the story of the Old Year that sank into the sea and is going to stay there until the end of time, when all the years have to march on top of the world so that everybody can say what they did each year. And the persons who do not want to say it will be devoured by white tigers that will descend from the clouds in bands.

"Will they devour me too, Indian?"

"You too, if you don't talk."

The story had been told to Concordio the Indian by Juan Pantaleón the Indian, the oldest one in the village, and Juan Pantaleón had heard it from Chumac the Indian, who was a medicine man, a wise medicine man. And thus the story had been repeated over and over so that it would be known. And the beginning of the story was that the Year, feeling old, was retiring. In the sky—who knows in what part because they can't be seen—hang two bags so big that the whole world would fit in them, and they're made of horsehair. In one bag are kept the years that have not yet reached Earth and in the other the years that have already left Earth. And the years there are bright, hard balls. And Time is the owner of the bags.

"And quite a few years ago," Concordio the Indian related, "nobody knows how many, a foolish Year decided to leave on the day that it shouldn't have instead of on the day that it should have. And the foolish Year, as soon as it saw that the hour was approaching, said: 'I'm off.'

And there was no one who expected it, no one who could stop it. Up above they didn't know until the next day that it was leaving, and no young year came in to take its turn. So the Old Year became round and, as no one helped it to position itself, tumbled and sank to the bottom of the sea. And nobody even found out about it. But then, all of a sudden, since the world had neither a New Year nor an Old Year, Time didn't know what to do. All the stars began to change position. And the Sun didn't come up and the Moon didn't come out, and people ran through the forests, shouting. And Time said that it could not send another Year until its turn came. And they searched and searched for the Year and the Year was nowhere to be found. And so everything in the world was topsy-turvy. And when another year did drop down, because its turn had come, Time learned that the foolish Year had sunk to the bottom of the sea, from which place no one can remove it. When it's the end and the thunderclaps and tigers come, then, yes, it'll be able to leave."

"And if it doesn't leave then?"

The Indian stared at me.

"Well, then, little girl, who knows what'll happen . . ."

After telling me his story Concordio the Indian fell silent. I decided to get up and leave. It was six o'clock.

I went as far as the big beach on the other side of the cove to take a look at the load of shrimp that was usually sold in the huts on the bank. I calmly began to bargain, bought what I wanted, took it—live, fresh, salty—and returned by the same path.

I reached the rocks. There, sitting on his heels, with his palm-leaf hat pushed onto the back of his neck, Concordio the Indian was waiting for the canoe that, as soon as night fell, his father Epifanio the Indian would paddle to the beach. The sun, which was going down and had almost dipped below the horizon, illuminated his figure from behind. In front of the Indian the cove stretched out to the open sea. The Indian continued to squat without moving.

Perhaps he was meditating on the fate of the year that, "on the day that it shouldn't have," had fallen into the sea.

The Weaver of Dreams

ROGELIA WAS A useless little girl. This was what her sisters and the schoolteacher said.

At school she would be asked to recite the lesson and she was so inattentive that she didn't know what she was being asked. And at home they would tell her to iron handkerchiefs, in order to learn little by little, and she would burn them; to serve the coffee in cups, and she would spill it on the tablecloth; to water the plants, and the water would fall to the ground.

"This child is very clumsy," said her sister Camila, who was very clever and very presumptuous.

"This child is stupid," added her sister Pepa.

"This child . . . you don't know whether she's learning or not learning," sighed the schoolteacher.

The worst thing was that Rogelia could not get the hang of tatting. Her grandmother, her sisters, and her aunts—all the women in her house—handled the shuttles with great skill and made lovely lace with stars, birds, and flowers, braiding all the fantasies with their thread. Rogelia liked that a lot. She would sit next to her grandmother with a pincushion, thread, and shuttles on her knees, and begin to dream about marvelous patterns. But so much did she dream about her patterns and with so much enthusiasm did she fancy them in her mind's eye that the shuttles clashed and tangled the thread, the pins fell to the floor, undoing the knots, and the work was turned upside down.

Rogelia would cry, ashamed, while her older sisters started on their reprimands.

"Lay out the tissue paper that we use to wrap our lacework," Camila would say to her. "You're useless for anything else."

And this happened to Rogelia every day.

55

ONE AFTERNOON SHE was leaning out of the window and saw, passing by the house, a very old woman who was looking up at the sky. Rogelia, who was a very well brought up little girl, ran to the door and went out into the street, because she thought the old woman was going to trip and fall down. But the old woman laughed and said to her:

"Don't worry. I look at the clouds. Afterwards I'm able to do some very pretty handiwork."

"What work do you do?" Rogelia asked her.

"I'm a weaver of dreams," the woman replied.

Those words fired Rogelia with enthusiasm.

"What a beautiful occupation!" she exclaimed, and then asked again. "What is your name, Señora?"

"My name is Gosvinda."

Rogelia would have liked to follow old Gosvinda, but she did not dare. She stayed in the doorway, watching her, and saw her continue all along the street and then exit the town and enter the forest.

From that day on, Rogelia thought only about the weaver of dreams. She was more and more distracted at school; she burned clothes more and more with the iron; she spilled water more frequently when watering the flowerpots; and she tangled the pins, shuttles, and thread more often when she sat next to her grandmother to do tatting.

"This child," said her sister Pepa one day, "will have to be sent to a boarding school. We'll see if they manage to teach her something."

"A place," added her sister Camila, "where she'll be kept locked up and punished."

"Where she won't be permitted to watch the clouds for hours on end," Pepa spoke out again.

"She's useless," offered her aunt.

Rogelia then said to her sisters:

"Since I have to learn something, I'm going to learn to weave dreams."

And her sisters laughed at her.

But Rogelia gathered in a cardboard box two changes of clothes, a jacket, and her rain boots, put on a bonnet that she had for holidays, went to give her grandmother a kiss, and set out.

ROGELIA LEFT THE town and arrived at the forest. The woods were dark because of the heavy forest canopy. Rogelia walked for a long time until she came across a clear meadow. In the meadow was a house with the sides painted pink and the windows painted green, and surrounded by yellow flowers. The house had seven chimneys from which escaped a pretty smoke that did not look like any other smoke, and was a different color in each chimney. Rogelia pushed the door, which was unlocked, and entered the house. From the kitchen you went up to a bedroom; from the bedroom you went up to the attic; and from the attic you saw the clouds and the faraway mountains. There, in the attic, old Gosvinda worked all day long, weaving dreams. The smoke of the dreams was what escaped through the chimneys.

On arriving at the attic, Rogelia said:

"Good morning, Señora Gosvinda."

It did not surprise the weaver to see the little girl.

"I knew you would come," she responded.

Rogelia glanced all around. She saw the distaffs and the looms with glass, gold, and silver threads, and with threads the color of emeralds and sapphires. In one corner there were twelve mice smoothing their whiskers.

"I've come to stay, if you'll let me," she said to Gosvinda. "I want to learn to weave dreams. At my house they say that I'm useless, but maybe I can learn such a pretty occupation."

Gosvinda told her that she could stay, and explained that she needed a little girl to help her because she had many commissions. People needed more and more dreams.

Rogelia stayed at the house in the forest. In the morning, very early, she would go up to the attic to arrange the threads on the looms and the bundles of fiber on the distaff. The threads were drawn through until forming the weft that the old weaver desired, and the wheel would spin faster and faster, creating a current of air that made the mice sneeze. During the day the cuckoos, and at nightfall the swifts, flew in and out of a window carrying in their bills the commissions given them by princes from royal palaces and by miners from their deep caves. All the men and women who knew the weaver commissioned dreams from her.

"There used to be seven of us weavers," Gosvinda told Rogelia. "But my companions retired to rest and I was left alone. They were older than I am. When I get tired and go away, there won't be anyone."

"And what will they do in the world?"

"They'll manufacture some pills in order to have synthetic dreams. And children will weave their dreams themselves."

Little by little Rogelia learned to make beautiful wefts of the color and shape of the clouds. She learned to retain the rainbow with songs and insert it in orange-colored dreams. She learned to weave pink and blue dreams for young people, and green ones to give hope to sick and sad people. And white dreams so that children could embroider them in colors.

"You're a very clever little girl," old Gosvinda said to her.

And Rogelia glowed with contentment.

"Oh!" she responded. "If those at my house saw me!"

"They would continue to consider you useless. If you say that you weave dreams, people will laugh at you."

The dreams, when they were woven, went out in a smoke lace, through the chimneys, and the wind carried them to faraway houses.

Rogelia also learned to sweep and to set pots on the fire. Every week a bear brought firewood to old Gosvinda, the rabbits took it upon themselves to bring vegetables, and the blackbirds arrived with fruit.

"What a beautiful house!" Rogelia would sigh.

ROGELIA LEARNED THE occupation so well that dreams no longer had secrets for her. Because she handled them so much, they no longer lodged in her head. She paid close attention to the fine, fragile threads, to the delicate wefts formed by the branches of the trees and the pattern of the clouds, and to the colors of the rainbow that settled over the sharp-pointed roof of the house. Rogelia never became confused anymore, because she no longer had the dreams in her head, but in her hands.

When I want a dream for myself, she thought, *I'll weave the most beautiful one that ever existed.*

One day old Gosvinda said to her:

"So that you'll know if this is truly your destiny you should conduct a test: go back to your home and work there."

Rogelia understood that she had to obey. She took her cardboard box and put on a dress that she had been weaving with remnants and adorning with the colors of the flowers.

ROGELIA ARRIVED AT her home, greeted everybody, and said that she had been learning to be clever. At first her sisters laughed at her, but Rogelia now had charmed hands. If she sat down to do tatting, the shuttles clicked like castanets and the threads were transformed into lace, with birds, flowers, and clouds on a background so white that it resembled a field of snow. If she watered the plants, she did not spill a drop. If she ironed, the clothes looked bright and new.

Everybody praised Rogelia. The yards of lace that she made were sought throughout the town. For big holidays people entrusted her with the decoration of their balconies.

But Rogelia could no longer live without dreams. Every day she went up to the highest part of the house to see if from there she could make out the smoke that rose from the chimneys of Gosvinda the weaver's house.

Once again Rogelia packed her cardboard box, said good-bye to everyone, and very early one morning set out for the forest.

"GOOD MORNING!" she said on entering the attic.

The weaver was sitting in her corner, and the mice held the bundles of fiber that she was putting on the distaffs.

"I knew you would come," she replied to Rogelia. "Now you'll stay here forever."

Rogelia stayed with old Gosvinda. She received the cuckoos and the swifts, fed the mice, helped the bear to unload the firewood, and prepared in their baskets the vegetables and fruits brought by the rabbits and the blackbirds. But most of all she wove and she wove. She wove the most complicated and difficult dreams, the ones that tired old Gosvinda. She attended to everything, because she had so many dreams in her hands that not a one remained in her head. So much did she love her dreams and so proud was she of her work that she never dared to hold them back.

Each year she went to the town to visit her grandmother, her sisters, and her aunt. She chatted with them and left again.

One day there knocked on the door of Gosvinda's house a very serious man who carried a big briefcase full of ledgers lined with black oilcloth. Rogelia came down from the attic to see what he wanted, and the man told her that he had come to find out who lived there and what her occupation was in order to note it in the tax ledger.

"Old Gosvinda and I live here," Rogelia explained to him, "and we're weavers of dreams."

The man checked his ledgers and said that that occupation did not appear on any list. He then cleared his throat and took his leave.

The Pirates of *The Terrible One*

The Gold and the Parrot

THE SHIP THAT broadcast on one side the expressive name of *The Terrible One* was among the last pirate ships that still plied the seas. The pirates who had not been captured barely managed to take any loot, because all captains, forewarned and carrying good cannons, were prepared to fight. Thus it was that little by little pirates had to withdraw to private life. They returned to their hometowns as if they were coming back from America, and they told no one that they had been pirates so as not to lose standing. They brought with them their share of the plunder, which was not much, and which scarcely provided them with enough for drinks in seamen's taverns. The lore about pirates' treasure was a fabulous myth, because all pirates, being distrustful, lost their treasure, as did those of *The Terrible One*, which is a very interesting tale and which never would have become known were it not for Desiderio, who sailed on that pirate vessel and afterwards could not hold his tongue.

The most complicated part of the division of those spoils turned out to be the determination of who would get the parrot. It's known that pirates always had a parrot with them, like a mascot, and all of them—except one, the lucky one—were very dissatisfied with the outcome of the drawing of lots. It was because of the parrots that the pirates, before they stopped being pirates, quarreled the most, more than over any island or any booty.

To give things in order: it happened that Desiderio, a boy of twelve who had gone to a secluded little beach to keep an eye on his father's boat, ran into the pirates. The pirates had come with neither hostile intentions nor the least desire to inflict harm. They had left *The Terrible One* in a cove in order to replenish their water supply. The Chinaman that they had on board—pirates always had a Chinese cook, because

60

no real pirate wants to work as one—informed them he couldn't continue cooking without water.

Were it not for this warning of the cook's, the pirates would have had no reason to find out if there was or wasn't water. Another of the things that everybody knows is that pirates, in order to be authentic pirates, could only drink rum from Jamaica, of which they always carried a very rich store. But in light of Chung the Chinese's warning, they decided to wait for nightfall to approach that solitary and secluded cove, at the ready to fill a few barrels with water at the first fountain or river that they came across. They took off their black caps with a skull painted in white, so that nobody could recognize them, and headed for land in two rowboats. But they did not bargain for Desiderio, a very curious boy.

Desiderio, after dragging his father's boat to the far end of the beach and tying it fast so that it wouldn't be washed out by the tide, was hurrying back toward the cove when he noticed a group of men and, as he was very curious, decided to investigate. He ran to the point of the cove, to the highest rock, and made out the sailing ship at a short distance, so short that, despite the approaching night, he could see on the bridge the figure of the captain with his wooden leg. *If he has a wooden leg and is on the bridge of a ship*, thought Desiderio, who was nobody's fool, *it means he's a pirate.* Therefore, when the group was happily returning, rolling barrels now filled with water, Desiderio went to meet them and, without thinking twice, said:

"So, pirates, eh?"

Whereupon Mac Mimpleton, a Scottish pirate with blond hair who was not fond of jokes, lifted him by the waist and said:

"So you won't go telling tales you're coming with us."

And whether he wanted to or not, Desiderio found himself turned into a cabin boy and apprentice pirate. The pirates of *The Terrible One* were already thinking about retiring. The bad times meant they were able to take fewer and fewer prizes. No ship allowed itself to be caught unprepared, and the heroic days of boarding a captured vessel with a knife between their teeth were already a distant memory. There was only the occasional assault to maintain the store of rum, and, when they set foot on land, Chung the Chinese would begin to complain that they were giving him less and less money for the purchase of provisions and that the marketplace had become very expensive.

"It's going to be necessary to throw this Chinaman overboard," said Mac Mimpleton, a man of decision.

The pirates, when they decided to retire, also decided to dig up their treasure. Good pirates, those of the great times of piracy, had a treasure. But they neither spent it nor kept it on their ships. That made no sense to a pirate. The treasure, which had to consist of gold doubloons seized in an assault on a powerful galleon, had to be buried. And buried in such a way that no one could ever find it.

To search for the site on a deserted island, to unload the treasure, to count the ounces and lock the chest, to seal it with wax stamped with a skull, all members of the crew being present, and to draw the map of the site with secret signs in order to deposit it in the captain's coffer—this is the most important task undertaken by pirates in their entire lives. The pirate who has done this can say that he has experienced the proudest moment of his life as a pirate.

The Terrible One sailed in a westerly heading with a favorable wind and, after many weeks of navigation, set a course for the Pacific in order to reach the archipelagos of the South Seas. The pirates spent the days drinking rum and singing songs of death and revenge that made one's hair stand on end. Only Desiderio and the Chinese cook drank water, and they were the only ones on that ship who worked. But Desiderio was content, because he was having a good time; he thought that, at long last, he was seeing the world, and since he heard talk of a treasure, he hoped that in the end they would give him something. At times he would dream about returning to his village rich.

The paper that the captain kept in his coffer read: "On the archipelago of the Snails, on the sixth island counting from the west, across from the cove that faces the south, at three o'clock in the afternoon the shade of a big palm tree that grows between the two cliffs falls on a sandy flower bed. At the foot of the sandy flower bed is a rocky stretch, from the center of which you have to measure twelve paces to the right and twenty back, in the direction of the palm tree. A man standing on that exact spot and facing east will count off fifty paces and come upon a pointed rock. Then he'll face north and count two hundred fifty paces, and there, in the earthy flower bed, covered with a stone slab, lies buried the treasure seized by the pirates of *The Terrible One*."

Desiderio was climbing up one of the masts when he heard the captain read the paper one night by the light of a resin torch, surrounded by all the pirates.

"That's an awful mess," said Desiderio.

"This is proof that we're first-rate pirates," responded the captain.

"It's going to be necessary to throw this boy overboard," said the Scotsman. "He's too curious."

The captain continued reading: "Of this treasure one half goes to the captain and the other half is to be divided among the crew without counting Chung the Chinese. Are you agreed?"

To a man they said yes, because, after all, that was the agreement.

But the bad part was when they set foot on the island. What happened there was what happened to all known pirates. They spent one day, then two days, and three days waiting until three o'clock in the afternoon, following the shadow of the palm tree, counting off paces, looking east, west, north, and south, and the site did not turn up.

"This isn't the island" was the opinion of some.

The captain ordered the rum hidden so that they would all have a clear head.

At the end of five days of checking they decided to dig at every spot on the island that wasn't rocky. They returned to the ship at night, exhausted and desperate, while the parrot would squawk its head off, saying: "This isn't the island, This isn't the island . . ."

At the end of fifteen days they became convinced that it was not the island they were searching for.

The pirates' odyssey—from island to island and having to end up digging the earth on all of them, leaving not a single inch unturned—was one of the most humiliating sagas recorded in the history of piracy. To make matters worse, the boldest ones began to protest.

"If we had a captain who knew about latitudes and longitudes . . . !"

And the parrot squawked its head off, shouting:

"He doesn't know the compass card!"

Because it was a very stuck-up parrot.

The captain had to write another piece of paper renouncing his privilege and accepting that the treasure, when it was found, would be divided into equal shares. Chung the Chinese argued that a stay of two months on tropical seas was not part of the contract, and declared that if he wasn't included as a coparticipant, he wasn't cooking. And he was included.

But it made no difference, because the treasure didn't turn up.

The pirates decided to seek consolation in the thought that the same thing would have happened to other great pirates. They took on a supply of coconuts, and with a barrel of rum bought a load of coral from the Malayans. Then they embarked on the return journey singing terrible war songs and drinking rum like madmen.

From America they sailed to the Madeira Islands, where some outfitters bought their ship along with the load of coral and arranged to have them taken to Cádiz.

Desiderio received twenty *duros*, a coral necklace, four pots from the Chinaman's kitchen, a cap that they let him keep as a memento, two knives that were magnificent for use in the woods, two ponchos, and four bottles of rum, with all of which he could return to his village like a king.

In addition, as the pirates were very annoyed with the mockery of the parrot, they decided to give him the bird too, because the Chinaman didn't want it.

And just in case he could use it for something, they handed over to him a secret document by virtue of which he could prove that he had sailed on *The Terrible One* and had participated in perilous ventures.

Martolán, Apprentice Magus

Story of the Starfish

HAVE YOU SEEN the starfish? All children have probably had occasion to see them. But what you surely have not noticed is the bad temper, the terrible anger shut up in them. There is no life-form living on top of the sand, submerged in saltwater, that is more unhappy with its fate. And the poor underwater stars have some reason to be, because they are like angels who have fallen into the water from the firmament.

Many years ago, many hundreds of years ago, seven very venerable and very elderly magi were charged with arranging the stars at night. They were seven wise magi and, as was only fitting for magi who devoted themselves to the study of heavenly bodies, they lived in Chaldea, where the king had had a tower built for them, a tower surrounded by gardens.

The magi of Chaldea studied the position of the stars and knew how they ought to be placed to preserve the preset order, so that the entire celestial vault would retain its appearance and no change would ensue. That was why the king ordered that a ladder be set up for them on the peak of Glass Mountain. Two hundred men transported the ladder and it was so long, so long, that when one end was placed at the foot of the mountain the other disappeared from view behind the last forest. It was so long that the slaves needed many days to stand it up straight while the king's bay horses pulled the silk cords tied to each rung. When, at last, it was straightened completely, the two silver hooks of the sidepieces were secured to the two horns of the Moon.

Only the seven magi could climb that ladder and no one else would have dared to do so. It took them many days to go up and many to return to Earth, but for that reason they were magi, and for that reason the king had entrusted them with the most important work in the kingdom, and paid them with big gold coins, and allowed them to live in the tower surrounded by gardens.

The magi went up, by turns, to arrange the stars so that the brightest ones would always shine over the royal palace. And if Princess Jasmine wished to contemplate the constellations in some special form, the magi, with diamond pincers, changed the arrangement of the stars and came up with tableaux and figures that produced astonishment throughout the kingdom. So the celestial vault functioned very well, although the seven magi had a lot of work and the climbs to the sky were becoming more and more arduous for them.

With the seven lived as many apprentices who were preparing to be magi, boys who studied, shut up in the tower, the strange sciences that only the magi knew. They studied all day long for twelve years, and afterwards the wise men taught them the magic formulas in order to be able to ascend the ladder without falling.

The smallest of the apprentices was named Martolán. He had been a student for only two years, but, since he turned out to be the quickest one, the learned magus Zalma, who was bothered somewhat by rheumatism, began to take him along as an assistant when it was his turn to go up to the clouds. Martolán climbed behind the old man carrying on a tray the diamond pincers, the goat-bristle brush made of hairs from goats on Glass Mountain, the only one that can brush the stars, and the pelt of a white chamois that should be picked up when the chamoix change skins during the August moon, and with which the blue enamel around the stars is polished.

Zalma the magus blindfolded Martolán to go up to the clouds so that the boy wouldn't get dizzy. When he was at the top, above stars and clouds, there was no longer danger, because the footing was more secure than on Earth. Martolán followed old Zalma and held out the tray to him, and, as the elderly magus was an artist, he would contemplate the perspective of constellations and begin to meditate like a sculptor standing in front of his work—first changing one star, then another. He would attach two more horses to Ursa Minor and add a tail seven yards long to Ursa Major. Princess Jasmine, from the highest window of her palace, clapped her hands with joy on seeing how the sky would change into such a marvelous form.

Thus it was that Martolán, finding himself so often in the midst of bright stars, experienced an intense desire to join in. And one time while the magus meditated, wondering if his work would be well executed, the apprentice seized the diamond pincers and gripped a star with all his strength.

Moving stars around and making color displays with their light is more difficult than it seems. Once it was wrested from its place in the appropriate constellation, the star came away from the diamond pincers and fell, tumbling and tumbling through clouds until disappearing in space.

"What a beautiful spectacle!" exclaimed Princess Jasmine, clapping. "Old Zalma has to be told to repeat it."

And no sooner had she finished saying so than a second and a third star tumbled like the first one, lighting up the atmosphere and shooting sparks on reaching Earth and plunging into the water of the sea.

When the magus realized that the stars were tumbling and disappearing, he began to rebuke Martolán and threatened to send him tumbling too, down all the rungs of the ladder.

"A star!" he said to him. "Do you realize what you've done? You've killed a star! The entire firmament will be up in arms at me."

But nothing happened, and when, eight days later, they reached Earth, the princess came to the tower of the seven magi.

"Great Zalma, the spectacle that you organized is the most beautiful one I've ever seen. I wish to see, again, how the stars tumble until falling in the sea and produce a shower of sparks like a live coal going out."

The stars that fell from Martolán's grasp had sunk in the ocean, and they shot sparks on hitting the water, like a piece of wood in flames or like a red-hot iron in a blacksmith's forge.

Thus it was that Zalma, refusing to assume the responsibility himself, allowed Martolán to change stars around from time to time and permitted some to fall from his grasp, lighting up the atmosphere until sinking in the sea.

And this went on for many years, until the apprentice became a full-fledged magus and learned the magic words in order to be able to climb the ladder alone to go up to the clouds. Then another apprentice accompanied him as an assistant and dropped some stars when he wanted to rearrange the order of the constellations.

And thus, one after another and little by little, many stars were extinguished in the sea. They flew into a rage on feeling their fire die out and, pallid and deflated, went down to the bottom to hide in the green algae.

Since then they have remained there on the bottom of the sea. They have lost their brilliance, but not their haughtiness. They have assumed the air of dethroned queens and hide so that no one will see them.

On clear nights they sometimes rise to the surface to gaze, filled with envy, at their sisters who have stayed up in the firmament.

Barú and the Giant

Story of the Divers of the Island of Manar

BARÚ SAT IN the boat with his feet dangling in the water while he took in the daily sight: the descent and ascent of the divers, flushed and gasping, from the surface to the bright sand on the bottom.

The men—naked except for their gloves, and with a small basket at their side—gathered on a rock as round as a mill wheel. Attached to a rope, they used a foothold that had been fashioned on the rock and descended to the sand at the bottom of the sea. They stayed submerged to collect, in the brief moments that their lungs could hold out, the pearl oysters that adhered to rocks and algae. They would come up and go back down again, and the boat would fill with wet mollusk shells that were covered with lustrous seaweed. Tireless and stopping from time to time only to fill their lungs with air, the divers swam up and down, and while the men who remained on board hauled in and released the ropes, they let out great yells in order to scare away the circling sharks.

This happened many years ago, on the coasts of the island of Manar, in the Indian Ocean.

Barú thought that the divers' work was beautiful: to enter the water with the rock as a platform and reach the sand on the bottom, and from there be able to contemplate the sky through the blue canopy of the water; to pick the big oysters from among the algae and the starfish, and to feel the excitement of the shark that approaches while they hoist the load from the boat. It seemed like fine work to Barú, but he knew it was so hard that only the king's slaves did it. He could not forget the men who fell on the beach in a pool of blood, their lungs having suddenly burst, or who were immobilized, with their limbs numbed forever as a result of having gone from the surface to the bottom time and time again.

Barú was the son of the overseer in charge of the boat. Barú was small and dark. He always went barefoot and, in his free time, liked to plunge into the sea from the rocks in order to practice diving. But for the better part of the day he helped his father; they had to unload the pearl oysters and set them out in the sun, on the esplanade. The shells opened in the warmth and, as the flesh separated, the pearls began to appear—white or black, lead-colored, or softly iridescent in mauve, green, blue, and gray. Pearls with a marvelous luster that reflected light and shadows.

Barú knew that the pearls all belonged to the king of Ceylon, and that, after many days of diving in order to bring the treasure of the bottom of the seas to the surface and so to augment the fabulous jewels of the crown, the slaves had to die. He also knew that the most extraordinary jewels ever collected by any sovereign were kept in the chests of the royal palace, and that when other kings and princes came to Ceylon they always turned green with envy before that wealth. He also knew that other slaves cut through mountains and bored tunnels to the center of the Earth to search for precious stones: diamonds, rubies, emeralds, and topazes. But Barú thought that the divers did the most terrible work.

ONE DAY BARÚ went out in his father's boat and the tide took him to a group of islands, off to the west, where nobody was accustomed to going because the islands were rocky and arid, and, according to the old people, inhabited by evil spirits. Barú pulled the boat ashore and, waiting for the tide to change, started strolling along the beach. Although still a child, he was a good sailor and had no fear of tackling the crossing by himself. He was walking very calmly, examining the island, when he ran into the Giant.

At that time, even though this occurred many years ago, the giants were already beginning to disappear and if there were any left nobody ever saw them, so for Barú it was a huge surprise to run into one of the biggest giants that have existed, one so tall that nothing less than a tree served as his walking stick, so tall that at his side Barú looked like a mouse.

"Good morning, Giant," he said.

"Good morning. Well, finally I have a visitor," responded the Giant.

"What are you doing here?" asked Barú.

"I live here," explained the Giant, "in that cave you see inside the rock."

And he invited Barú to his cave. It was an enormous cave with tree trunks that the Giant had fashioned into a seat and a bed. Sturdy chests made of knotty wood stood flush against the rock walls.

"You don't know," continued explaining the Giant, "that just as gnomes are charged with penetrating the bowels of the Earth and the most beautiful gemstones belong to them, giants have had, for many hundreds of years, the privilege of finding on the bottom of the sea the most beautiful pearls that have ever been seen. The good pearls are never found by people. They're ours. We know where they are, and we're the owners of the sands in which they grow."

"What do you do with the pearls, Giant?"

"Sometimes ships come from the Persian Gulf, where all the merchants of Asia gather; other times they even come from China and Japan, and the Mediterranean, because the pearls from my coasts are more valuable than any others in the world. With them the crowns of queens and princesses are made, and when the goldsmiths of Florence receive a commission from the king of France, or those of Venice to make a brooch for the doge's wife, they send merchants requesting the loveliest pearls, the ones with a pink tint, the ones that are iridescent in gold or gray, the ones that have such extraordinary luster that they glow in the dark. That's why I live here alone. Because if I leave, who will bring up these pearls? What will the jewelers of Europe do? With each voyage they send me sealed parchments saying: 'Ask us for gold and silver and all that you wish, but send us your pearls.'"

"But, Giant," said Barú, "over on Manar, where I live, marvelous pearls are also gathered."

The Giant then opened a chest, and Barú thought he would faint from astonishment because he had never seen pearls like those. Round or like teardrops, brilliant like stars, and in every color and hue to be found in the sea.

Afterwards the Giant took Barú under his arm, went out to the beach, and started walking in the water. His hand swept the bottom, and so long as he walked, the waves did not cover it up.

"I know the pearl oysters," he said, "that's our first secret. And I find them in whatever nook they're hidden."

"Do you know, Giant, the hardships that men undergo to gather pearls, and how the slaves who devote themselves to such a terrible pursuit die?"

"Yes, I do, which is why I allow them to utilize the entire coast. I have enough with my islands. Sometimes I go from one island to another, at low tide, and fill so many sacks that the beach glistens when I spread the shells in the sun. I don't want anyone to know me, because the king of Ceylon would covet my pearls and . . . why do I need the king of Ceylon? The ships from the Persian Gulf and Europe bring me provisions and treats. My boots for rock climbing are sewn by the best harness maker in Genoa, and in Spain they weave blankets specially for my bed. A confectioner in Paris sends me sweets and jams, and everybody remembers me. Only I and two other giants— one who's in Marosakia and another in Analalasa—take pearls from the world's seas. When I grow tired and leave, there'll be no one in the Indian Ocean."

Barú was thinking about a great idea that had occurred to him and kept quiet. The Giant went back to the cave with him and said:

"Since you're the first child I've seen in a long time, I want to give you a gift with the condition that you tell no one about it. Choose, from my chests, the pearl you like best."

"I'm thinking, Giant," responded Barú, "that with a handful of these pearls you could set free all the king's slaves. If you go before the king and offer to give him a few pearls each year, he'll no longer want the slaves to die diving to the bottom of the sea, because all the pearls they bring up will look dull compared with yours."

"I don't want to have dealings with the king of Ceylon. He's covetous and would want to take possession of everything."

"He can't become your enemy, because only you can obtain these pearls, and the slaves'll be so grateful that they'll come to keep you company and sing and dance to cheer you. Everybody will love you, Giant."

Giants are kind and fond of doing favors. So big, so big, and they get excited very easily and suffer when they see misfortune. As a result, the Giant, who was not accustomed to thinking much about things, hoisted one very full chest on one shoulder and Barú's boat, with Barú in it, on the other, and headed out into the sea and walked until he reached the island of Manar.

NO ONE IN the country recalled an occurrence like the one when the Giant appeared at the king's palace to ask for the freedom of the slaves. The court treasurer set a price of twelve pearls a head, and the prime minister added an annual tax that the Giant had to pay to the king for as long as he remained on the islands to the west of Manar. The sovereign for his part pledged not to use more slaves for such terrible work, and the Giant offered to come every now and then to bring up some of the small pearls, which now seemed so small that the king decided they should be earmarked for gifts to ambassadors from other countries and for the amusement of the princesses.

The Giant was invited to eat at the king's palace. He devoured forty puff pastries, twenty platters of sweetened egg yolk strands, one hundred three tarts, six jars of jam, and one silver bucketful of rice pudding. Since the days of Tom Thumb giants have been vegetarians.

So overjoyed were the slaves that each one bought a bottle of anisette and spent eight days asleep in a hammock. Barú asked his father's permission to go off to the Giant's island, and there he began to reflect that if gnomes were good they would be able to buy the freedom of the slaves who toiled in the mines. But gnomes have a worse temper than giants, and that was going to take some doing on Barú's part.

The Conceited Buzzard

The Story of an Indian Woman

ALTAGRACIA THE INDIAN, who was such an old woman that no one remembered her age, told me this story one day while she was peeling prickly pears by the doorway of her hut.

Altagracia the Indian dressed entirely in white and tied the plaits of her hair with colored ribbons. Although she was very old, she squatted easily hour after hour and peeled prickly pears without being stuck by a single thorn.

Above that hut surrounded by palm trees, buzzards flew around and around, as they always fly around looking for something to devour. Buzzards have the misfortune of being ugly, so much so that only with difficulty would another bird be their equal; and since they're big, and have a horrible, bare neck that stands out over dull, black plumage, the poor things attract more attention.

What's bad is that buzzards, beside being ugly, are very conceited and seek to eclipse the lovely birds that live deep in the forests. This is what Altagracia the Indian woman related to me, and she declares that this a true story.

Life in a Forest

BUZZARDS LIVE IN cities and retire at nightfall, forming a black line on jetties and walls until dawn awakens them. But in other times they lived in the forest, in the dense woods, and on the banks of rivers where monkeys frolicked. There the splendid birds of paradise and peacocks, along with hummingbirds and mockingbirds and parakeets and cockatoos, filled the big trees with the color of their feathers and the harmony of their warbles. The trees shook with birds that went

73

up and down, amidst the dense crowns, to sing in the sun above the shaded forest and under the blue sky.

The buzzards also lived there. Ugly and smelly, their caws pervading the air, they were the most unfortunate of the winged inhabitants of the forest. But they did not see it that way. No sooner did the bald heads of their young peek out of the nest than their parents fished for compliments from the monkeys that jumped from branch to branch.

"Mister Monkey, have you seen what beautiful children we've brought into the world?"

Monkeys understand very little of beauty and do not wish to be on the outs with anyone. While they swing on a liana and somersault from one tree to another over water packed with crocodiles, they scarcely have time to turn around.

"Lovely, Mister Buzzard . . ."

And they forgot about the repulsive little creatures that were screeching inside the nest.

When, on its slow flight, one of the beautiful birds stopped at his tree, the buzzard puffed up and, cawing loudly, would say:

"Brother, have you seen what beautiful chicks?"

The bird would look at them and, without answering him, extend its wings so that the loveliest colors of the rainbow would show on its feathers in the reflection of the sun that filtered through the thick growth.

The buzzards were not mortified by the prettiness of the others because they did not see it. If it was a mockingbird that came around to show off its marvelous singing, the buzzard would turn to his chicks and say:

"Don't sing now, because your voice is more beautiful and will outshine the mockingbird's."

The Falcon and the Sparrow Hawk Receive a Visitor

ALL THE BIRDS in the forest made fun of the buzzards. While the ones with the red, blue, green, and gold of fire, or marvelous combinations of colors, sang their joy from daybreak on and flew to the clearings in search of sweet, ripe, juicy fruit, the buzzards slowly followed the smell of carrion to contend for it with the voracious jackals.

One day the eggs of all the nests in the forest opened to make way for the chicks, which in a few short weeks were covered with yellow down, or lightly colored feathers, and stretched out in jaunty and graceful fashion, eager to fly. All the birds had hidden their nests in the branches of trees, in the holes of the trunks, and between the moss and lianas, because they feared the falcon and sparrow hawk that continually circled over the forests.

When the buzzards in the nest began to grow, the big buzzard decided to assure their protection. He put on formal attire, in which he looked more ridiculous and more ugly, and, crossing the forest and the meadows cleared of vegetation, came to the open space near the mountains and kept going until he reached the high peak that over-looked the plain, the forest, the woods, and the river. There he met the falcon, who was serious and bloated, digesting as he was a rabbit.

"Mister Falcon," said the buzzard, removing his derby, "although I recognize my inferior standing, I should explain that I belong to your strain of birds of prey. I'm not like those simple birds in the forest. Therefore, in the name of our kinship, I make bold to ask protection of you for my children who are still in the nest. I beg you not to attack them."

"What are your young like?"

"The most beautiful chicks that you'll see, with the most sonorous singing—those are my young."

"Very well," said the falcon, who at the time could not even move. "I'll respect your young. But talk to the sparrow hawk lest he mistake them."

So the buzzard went and talked to the sparrow hawk and repeated what he had said to the falcon, and afterwards did not worry again. The big buzzards left their young in the nest to go in search of carrion, and smugly strutted on the branches of their tree, saying that, as they were friends of the falcon and sparrow hawk, their nest was free from attacks.

The Falcon's Mistake

AND ONE FINE day all the little buzzards went missing from the nest. When the big pair returned from their forays they found the entire forest silent, with all the other birds in their hiding places, terrified. The hummingbird and the mockingbird peeked their heads out to explain to them that the falcon had been flying over the forest while their young were cawing and making a racket in the nest, and that it had swooped down and snatched two chicks, carrying them off in its beak and talons. In the bend of a branch they found the third chick half scared to death.

"And thus it was," continued Altagracia the Indian woman, "that the buzzard went to call the falcon to account, and the falcon asked:

"'But, which ones were your young?'

"'Like this chick I've brought here for you to see,' and opening the feathers between his wings he revealed a frightful, repulsive little creature that began to caw until it became hoarse."

Falcons don't know how to laugh. Altagracia, who knows all the details of this story, assured me that they're serious, cruel birds that forebode wars. If they did know how to laugh, the falcon would have laughed a great deal at the buzzard's vanity.

Move to the City

AS A CONSEQUENCE of that scorn, the two buzzards and their chick left the forest, and all the buzzards of other forests followed suit. They left the lovely old trees, from which spring the aromatic gums, and the fresh, shaded forest; the riverbank alive with the chatter of monkeys; the plains covered with red, yellow, blue, and every other color of flower; and the silvery water, sometimes still, sometimes frothy from a swift flow. They left the marvelous world of birds and went off to dusty, asphalted towns.

Each evening they go for a stroll in formal attire, looking very serious as they hop and remove their derbies from their bald heads with ridiculous gravity. People ignore them because they're no good for singing and you can't use their feathers; and since, in order to fill their filthy stomachs, they clean up the city every morning, people also let them live in peace.

And Altagracia says that they are more and more conceited and that they parade around so contentedly because they still believe that they're the loveliest birds in the world.

The Little Girl and the Sea

THE SAILOR, ON heading toward his boat, said to the little girl:

"Close the doors and don't let the Sea in."

The Sea wanted to enter the house as soon as night fell. His waves came up the sand chanting in a soft voice, and, as they washed over the stones on the beach, they would then continue in a loud voice, pounding the rocks tirelessly. And their chant at the foot of the house was always the same: "Let me in . . . ! Let me in . . . !"

"Let me in," the Sea would say to the little girl. "I come from America and I'm very tired; I covered many miles under the sun and the moon; I supported many boats on my shoulders and I opened up to receive the placement of nets. I'm tired. I left Cuba filled with warmth and now I'm shaking with cold here. Let me in . . ."

The house sat on top of the rocks and the little girl leaned out of the window in order to hear the Sea's words.

"Why don't we let him in?" she would ask her father, the fisherman.

"Because the Sea tells lies. He's neither tired nor cold. He's strong, stronger than land and than fire. If he was allowed to reach land and fire, fire would be extinguished and land scorched; green grass would turn yellow and everything would be covered with salt. The Sea wants to enter the house in order to go out into the countryside and drown the flowers and trees. He wants to take us down to the bottom of his domains. The Sea lies, because he wants to kill us."

That night, when the fisherman left, the little girl leaned out of the window to listen to the chant of the waves pounding the rocks: "Let me in . . . ! Let me in . . . !" And when he saw the little girl at the window the Sea began to relate his hardships to her.

"The islands are very heavy for me. I'm old and I don't know how I'll be able to hold them up. I have to let them sink."

"Don't let them sink, Sea," the little girl said to him. "The islands have paper houses and little goats that climb their mountains; they

77

have green meadows and white flowers; they have pine trees and palm trees . . . Don't let them sink."

"In other countries," the Sea continued saying, "they push me back, they hem me in with walls, and they cover the sand that belongs to me with earth. They steal my domains to build cities, and they only let me come in through canals where I'm confined like in a jail. I'm left without my beaches to rest and can't reach my coasts with the waves. I'm going to have to summon my waves from the bottom and rise up over the cities and over the canals."

"Don't rise up, Sea," said the little girl. "In the canals there are wooden boats painted in many colors, and on the boats live the wives of the sailors and on the decks they hang, out in the sun, their children's clothes. Alongside the canals there are men who play the accordion and old sailors who smoke their pipes. In the cities, Sea, the ones that were built on the sands that were taken from you, there are many streets and many squares, and piers filled with people that wait for the steamships that you bring from Asia and Africa, loaded with cinnamon, elephants, and monkeys, and little blacks dressed in yellow. Don't rise up over the cities."

And the Sea repeated:

"I'm tired . . . Let me in . . ."

"I can't let you in, Sea. My father, who's a sailor and spends days and nights navigating over your waves, tells me that we can't let you in, that you're an old liar. He tells me that you'll enter the house and go out into the countryside and cover it all up, that you'll extinguish our fire in the fireplace and the flame that burns in the small lamp in front of the Blessed Virgin. So you see . . . You'll sink the house, crush the flowers, and topple the trees. You're stronger than we are. I can't let you in, Sea, I can't."

But the Sea kept pounding the rocks and chanting:

"Let me in . . . ! Let me in . . . ! Let me in to see your fire, little girl. I can't see the sailors' fire. The red-hot boilers in the holds of ships navigate inside of me; I pound so that they'll let me reach them, and they don't let me. I, on the other hand, give the fires of my algae to the sailors, I make a gift of my fishes to them, and I have the wind come to push their sails."

"I can't, Sea . . . "

But the little girl felt pity for the tired, old Sea.

"If I open the door, will you leave when I tell you to?"

"I'll leave when you tell me to."

"You won't put out the fire on the logs? You won't put out the flame that's burning in the oil?"

"I'll warm myself by the logs and won't put out the flame."

The little girl left the house and approached the Sea. She leaned over the waves that continued to chant on the rocks and opened the wicket of studded wood that separated the rocks from land. The Sea, then, rolled in like a tongue of foam, embraced the little girl, and carried her off with him. The Sea enveloped her so that she wouldn't be bashed against the rocks, and carried her off, raised up on his shoulders, so that the Moon could see her.

The waves, washing over the rocks, chanted: "The little girl belongs to the Sea . . . The little girl belongs to the Sea . . ."

The Sea then engulfed the little girl and sank her among the silvery fishes and drowned stars.

AT DAWN THE Sea feared the arrival of the fisherman. He gathered the little girl in his green arms, lifted her from his sandy bottom, and raised her so that she would receive the first rays of the sun. The Sea rode over himself, trampling his waves, always with the little girl in his arms. He entered by the open wicket, swept the land, passed through the door to the house, and left the little girl laid out on her bed, on top of the flowery bedspread. Afterwards the Sea withdrew, sank between the rocks, and, as it was already daytime, stopped chanting.

The fisherman returned from the pier wrapped in yellow oilskin, carrying his flat basket full of fishes under his arm. He saw the extinguished fireplace and the flame of the burning lamp. He saw each thing in its place: the paper flowers on the bureau; the straw chairs around the table; the calendar hanging on the wall; and the blessed palm leaf tied above the little girl's bed. And on the bed, stretched out, the little girl.

But she was dead.

Karlantán and Prince Atal's Pearls

Story of the Kingdom That Had No Sea

IN A REMOTE country, and in times still more remote, the great sovereign Tayul ruled over millions of vassals. The king's castle stood atop a mountain, over a crest of rocks. It was a magnificent palace, surrounded by gardens in which the king had the most beautiful of flowers grown for the pleasure of Princess Karlantán, his only child. The royal forests, inhabited by deer, pheasants, and birds of paradise, stretched out beyond the gardens. On the broad lakes, which were covered with swans and water lilies, boats bobbed gently, boats in which the princess liked to take a ride in the afternoon.

The entire palace was sumptuous and luxurious, but from it one could not see the sea. Neither from the palace nor from any part of the country. The sea was much farther away, beyond the borders of Tuhán. In Tuhán there were rivers of great volume on which fishermen's boats and passengers' sailing ships navigated; there were rivers of little volume that flowed through meadows and drove windmills; there were canals that irrigated the land where trees and wheat grew; and there were blue lakes in the mountains. But no one, in that kingdom, knew what the sea was.

All the borders were surrounded by forests that formed a belt defending Tayul's possessions. Every sixty miles the king had ordered the construction of a fort from which ten lookouts watched the horizon with long telescopes, and trained eagles flew over the tops in order to warn, in case of attack, the thousand warriors who guarded each fort. It was necessary for King Tayul to take these measures because his territory was very rich and could excite the greed of neighboring kings.

Tuhán was a powerful, beautiful, fertile country. But from it one could not see the sea.

When the royal jewelers labored to set jewels in crowns, they sent for diamonds, emeralds, rubies, and all the precious stones from the royal mines, in which dozens of men descended into the bowels of the earth to toil. Tayul and Karlantán could don the most beautiful diadems and gemstone-studded cloaks that any sovereign could ever have been able to show off. But never, glittering on satin or mounted on gold and platinum filigree, had pearls been known in the palace of Tuhán.

Until one day when one of the neighboring princes, who wished to gain Tayul's friendship, sent his ambassador with a dazzling gift: a big rock crystal vase filled with pearls, the loveliest pearls that anyone had seen.

Neither the people who lived on the coral islands of the warm seas, where pearls reach full development like smooth, polished cherries, nor the captains from whose boats black slaves descended to the bottom of the seas to rob the secret from the nacre shells had seen their like. There were black and white pearls, enormous pear-shaped pearls, and round pearls like grapes picked from a sun-drenched bunch. Pearls that glittered in the reflection of light, pearls with a wondrous orient that locked in the mystery of the sea, the brightness of the moon, and the movement of the goldfish among the shells that rest on the white sand and phosphorescent algae.

The king received the big crystal vase and let the precious little balls run through his fingers.

"Have them put," he ordered, "on the terrace of the first garden, on the tea roses and the blue lilies. They'll glisten among the leaves with the dew and be more beautiful than the flowers."

But Princess Karlantán, who was given to pondering things, became saddened when she saw the pearls. She understood that such a marvel came from some distant and strange place, completely unknown in the land of Tuhán; that the pearls, like the diamonds, did not issue from mines in deep holes beneath the surface, nor did they grow in the forests, nor did they originate in the flowing current of rivers, where silvery trout and coral salmon swam. Neither were they found floating in the water lily-covered lakes, nor did they sway among the reeds on the bottom of irrigation channels, nor did they spring from the corolla of flowers.

The princess understood that, far from the kingdom of Tuhán, there existed marvelous places that were strange for her, and the more she contemplated the pearls the more saddened she became.

Tayul then called together the savants of the kingdom.

"It is necessary," he said to them, "that you study this matter and provide me with an answer. The princess wishes to know the origin of the beautiful bright balls that Prince Atal has sent me."

There were twelve savants in Tuhán, to whom the king's treasurer each year gave a bag of gold coins so that they could devote themselves to the terrible and difficult sciences. Thus the astronomers, alchemists, and physicists, necromancers, fortune-tellers, and herbalists—all those who researched the nature of animals and plants in enormous cabalistic tomes—inquired into the destiny of the kingdom or looked for the philosophers' stone. All of them, absolutely all of them, shut themselves up in their immense studies to carry out the king's order. At the end of eight days they requested an audience.

Tayul received them in the third salon of the palace's left wing, where he customarily listened to scientific addresses. He was seated on his damask-covered throne, and the princess occupied an ivory and lignum vitae throne.

"Let us see," said the king. "What is it that you have ascertained?"

"Your Majesty," replied Sakán, the astronomer, who was the first in the semicircle of savants and at whom the king pointed his finger, "the beautiful bright balls that were given as a gift to Your Majesty by Prince Atal are formed by the gases of the Moon, which revolve in space, locking light in. When the gases become concentrated—in some countries located to the south, beyond the big blue lakes—those little balls fall like rain and have no value at all."

The king let the next savant speak.

"Your Majesty," said the latter, "all those who want to know the ancient and occult science that I decipher in my books will be in a position to understand that the bright little balls, whose origin Your Highness wishes to know, come from strange trees in a country located many miles to the north, in which the sun never shines but the stars always glitter. If Your Majesty gives his permission, I shall devote another week to deciphering more details."

The king called upon a third savant.

"Your Majesty, after meditating these past eight days and their corresponding nights, I believe I can assure you that Prince Atal's gift is composed of the teeth of some strange animals that are discussed in alchemy treatises, and that live only in the depths of the forests of the country located at the other end of the Earth."

The great Poká, a wealthy, powerful savant who held the post of adviser to the king and was, therefore, haughty and vain, asked permission to intervene.

"I ask Your Majesty," he said, "to have these ignoramuses expelled from the kingdom. There is no doubt, and everybody should know it, that the bright little balls that we do not possess in our country are nothing but the eggs of some giant butterflies that have glass bodies."

"They are," shouted a botanist, "the seeds of a mountain tree, hardened in the snow."

"He lies, Your Majesty!" the necromancer began to yell.

But the princess begged the king to dismiss the twelve savants. The king then summoned the halberdiers. The latter pounded the floor so that the guards would enter and alert the master of ceremonies, the only one who knew the form of protocol whereby the savants ought to be dismissed from the royal presence.

When they had left and their shouts were no longer heard, the princess ordered a glass of water with orange blossom, honey, and lemon-flavored sugar paste.

"The savants that the crown supports," she said to the king, "are useless. The upshot of reading books they don't understand is that they've turned stupid. And they're getting more and more stupid because they're convinced that they're right."

As a result of all this the princess continued to be saddened when she went out to the terrace of the first garden and contemplated the pearls, bright with dew, whose origin no one could decipher. The savants had shut themselves up to proceed with their studies and spent another entire week bent over parchments or meditating before their retorts. But when they requested an audience a second time, the princess refused to⁻ listen to them.

One of the master jeweler's apprentices, who was a very clever craftsman, began, after asking the king's permission, to drill holes in the pearls and string them together in big necklaces so that the princess, when adorning herself with them, would forget her capricious desire, but the princess became more saddened each time that her maid covered her neck and bust with the bright, heavy strings that glistened on her dress.

One day, when Karlantán was strolling along the eighth terrace of the fourth garden, in which the rarest orchids grew, and pondering her distress at not being able to learn where the pearls grew or to decipher the mystery of their origin, she saw her wet nurse climbing the marble steps. The wet nurse climbed with great difficulty, because she was very stout and was weighed down with a big basket.

The princess's wet nurse no longer lived in the royal palace, because Karlantán was not like other silly princesses who are afraid of the night

or want the wet nurse to tell them stories. Felicidad the wet nurse
lived in her country house and came on a visit to the palace only twice
a year. But whenever the princess fell ill with a cold, or became sad,
the master of ceremonies, who knew how everything was to be done,
sent a messenger to alert Felicidad the wet nurse.

Princess Karlantán showed her the beautiful strings of pearls that
hung from her neck.

"Nobody in the entire kingdom, Wet Nurse—neither the savants
nor the masters—can tell me where these balls come from, in what
place they grow, and where that country is."

The wet nurse was a very prudent and very clever woman, and
thought a while before responding.

"Why are you upset, Princess? What does it matter to you to unravel
the mystery?"

"It's the only thing we don't know in this palace," said the princess.
"Up till now the savants discovered everything."

As she listened to this, the wet nurse began to laugh. Karlantán
could not get angry, because it is known that wet nurses are the only
ones who have the right to indulge in such confidences with princesses
and queens.

"The savants don't discover anything, Princess. The twelve palace
savants are a pack of fools. What's happening is that just because
things are seen every day, it seems to you that they're known and
that they hold no secrets. Let's see. Do the savants know why the
cuckoo lays its eggs in another bird's nest? Do they know whether
the Sun hides when the day goes away or whether the day goes away
when the Sun hides? Do they know which of its two horns point up
when the Moon begins to draw itself in?"

The princess was amazed.

"It's true, Wet Nurse. I had never thought about that."

"Have you thought," she asked, showing her a honeycomb, "about
where this comes from?"

"The truth, Wet Nurse . . ."

"Tell the king to gather all the savants, and I'll bet them one hundred
whacks with a stick that they don't know."

The savants, who claimed to know everything from the confinement
of the big rooms of their towers, studied the honeycomb carefully and
told the king that they needed eight days of meditation to decide where
that soft, golden, sticky, sweet paste came from.

The princess laughed, making fun of the savants, while the master
of ceremonies made them leave the royal presence. Afterwards she

asked her wet nurse to bring a beehive to be installed in one corner of her gardens, and so much was she entertained on seeing the bees work that she forgot about the origin of pearls.

One day Prince Atal—who was returning from a tour of the islands that were the possession of the king, his father—paid a courtesy call at the palace of Tuhán, and explained to King Tayul and Princess Karlantán how the slaves brought from the islands of the South immersed themselves in the sea, with both feet held fast on a big stone that was hitched to a rope, thus to descend to the depths in which the nacre shells envelop the marvelous pearls.

But nobody could recall any of that, because the great Poká, savant and adviser to the king, had already taken the precaution of recording in the Annals of the Crown that, in year XV of the reign of Tayul, a gift of homage from Prince Atal had arrived at the royal palace, a gift that consisted in hundreds of little balls, white and black, bright and hard, that, given over to the scrutiny of the savants, turned out to be the eggs of a gigantic butterfly with a glass body, and this butterfly, which descends from snow-covered mountains, is found in the meadows of some countries only thirteen days of the year.

All of which was written down by five clerks on yellow parchments that were put in chest XXVII of Archive VIII of the Crown.

The Garden with Seven Gates

(Dialogue for the Stage)

A vacant lot by a crossroads. At the back there is a partially demolished weed-covered wall with an open space at one end, to the right of the spectator. The entire lot, which in another time was perhaps a field or a garden, looks abandoned; the only thing there is a stone bench. Sitting on it is old Marconia, a woman who, more than old, is aged; she's dressed poorly, in light-colored clothes, and in a picturesque manner. Her white hair falls over her forehead in locks. She has a happy expression that contrasts with her miserable appearance.

Félix and little Adrián enter from the left. The older of these two boys is twelve, and the younger, who is very sickly, is ten or eleven. Both are dressed very modestly, in outfits like the uniforms worn at charitable institutions. They're carrying, slung over their backs and held by leather straps, black oilcloth schoolbags.

ADRIÁN.	Good afternoon!
MARCONIA.	Good afternoon! Where are you coming from?
FÉLIX.	We're not coming . . . We're going . . .
MARCONIA.	Where're you going?
FÉLIX.	To the sea.
MARCONIA.	The sea is very far away. You'll have to walk three days and three nights in order to reach the sea.
FÉLIX.	We'll walk three days and three nights . . . But, no . . . ! When we get to the river we'll ask the boatman to ferry us across to the other bank and that way we'll save a lot of time.
ADRIÁN.	We don't have the money to pay for the boat.
MARCONIA.	If you don't have the money, the boatman will refuse to ferry you across.

Félix.	We'll take a raft, one of the rafts that are always moored to the pier, and we'll paddle it with an oar.
Marconia.	If you take a raft the boatman will catch up with you, make you return to land, and turn you in to the watchman to be punished.
Félix.	We'll take it when the boatman won't see us.
Marconia.	He'll see you. He's always on the river. He sees everything that happens on its banks . . . and, besides, rafts are treacherous, they can flip, the current can sweep you along. You'll die by drowning.
Félix.	We won't take a raft; we'll walk. And, when we reach the sea, we'll board a big steamship . . .
Adrián.	We don't have the money to pay for the steamship . . .
Marconia.	If you don't have the money, the captain will lock you up in the hold; he'll make you work shoveling coal into the burning boilers. You'll die overcome by fire.
Félix.	Stokers don't die. They tend the fire in the boilers with their shovels by listening to the steam engine that drives the ship. And the ships travel quickly, belching smoke from their chimneys. Stokers don't die, they're content . . .
Adrián.	But we're not stokers . . .
Félix.	Don't be silly! You think he's going to give us such an important job to do? The captain doesn't bother with children. He walks back and forth on the deck smoking his pipe. He has one sailor at his side with a compass and another with a flag in order to know the direction of the wind. When he gets tired of walking he goes to his cabin. He has a monkey dressed in yellow and a barrel of rum. He sits down to drink the rum, the monkey climbs up on his shoulder, and there the captain stays, carefree, without anyone coming in to disturb him. Nobody'll say a thing to us. We'll become friends with the cabin boy and climb the rope ladder with him, the one to see if land can be sighted.
Marconia.	The sailors'll make you clean the bottom of the ship, and the rats'll bite you . . . If you don't do a good job of cleaning they'll flog you with a whip that has seven lashes.
Félix.	Sailors don't have a whip. They only have a parrot. Besides, they're always jolly. When they're finished working they sit together on the deck and sing.
Marconia.	There's no end to work on ships. Don't go! Stay here . . . I'll show you my garden.

FÉLIX.   What do we care about your garden?

MARCONIA.   It's the most beautiful garden you've ever seen. What's your
              name?

FÉLIX.   My name is Félix. And this is little Adrián.

MARCONIA.   No, he's a little prince.

              *(During the dialogue between Félix and old Marconia,
              little Adrián has been attentive and frightened. On
              hearing these words he cheers up.)*

ADRIÁN.   How do you know?

FÉLIX.   She's crazy. Princes don't go to an orphan asylum.

ADRIÁN.   How do you know? I was told once that I was a prince
              . . .

MARCONIA.   Old Marconia knows everything.

FÉLIX.   That's your name? It's as odd as you are. But you don't
              know anything. He's not a prince.

ADRIÁN.   Yes, Félix, maybe I am a prince. I'm going to stay in old
              Marconia's garden. Princes are always in a garden.

FÉLIX.   Princes are in their houses, which are palaces. You were
              in an orphan asylum and if you're caught you'll return to
              it. Let's go. We're wasting time . . .

MARCONIA.   First you have to see my garden . . .

FÉLIX.   Is it very far . . . ?

MARCONIA.   No . . .

FÉLIX.   Where is it . . . ?

              *(Marconia makes a gesture with her hands, like taking
              in the lot.)*

MARCONIA.   Here . . . It was here! The painter took it with him, but
              he's going to bring it back. The wind had made the apple
              tree's flowers fall and the dust dulled the foliage. The painter
              passed by and I said to him: "Paint my garden. Paint its
              flowers and leaves, and also the grass, and give it a fountain
              so that I can water it . . ." And he responded: "I need a
              big easel and many brushes and colors. I'll take your garden
              and bring it back to you when I'm finished."

FÉLIX.   You're a liar, old Marconia!

MARCONIA.   No, little boy, I'm not a liar . . .

FÉLIX.   Who's ever seen anybody take a garden? Thieves take gold
              and silver, banknotes and jewelry; they take an automobile
              and maybe even a plane or a train . . . But a garden
              . . . Who takes a garden?

MARCONIA.   But it wasn't thieves, it was the painter . . .

FÉLIX.   Nobody can take a garden.

MARCONIA.   The painter can, he can take it and bring it back. The painter, do you understand, can put trees, houses, and people wherever he wants to . . .

FÉLIX.   You've drunk anisette, old Marconia. Your head's not working right.

MARCONIA.   No, little boy, I haven't drunk anisette . . . I don't have money . . . Look, no money. *(Inside her skirt pocket is what looks like a watch fob, and from it she withdraws a very small old satin purse.)* I never have money. It's good to drink a little glass of anisette, or of that green liqueur that's so sweet . . . it's good, once in a while . . . but I can't. One day I saw the confectioner's wife in the street. She was smartly dressed in her big hat and shawl . . . I said to her: "Congratulations, Señora Hortensia!" It's always good to wish people well . . . And she said to me: "How do you know that it's my birthday?" And she took me to the confectionery, invited me to have a piece of cake, and afterwards gave me a little glass of anisette . . . But that was one day, I don't know when, a long time ago.

FÉLIX.   If you're not a liar and didn't drink anisette, then you must be crazy.

ADRIÁN.   She's not crazy, Félix. She has a garden, she's telling you that.

MARCONIA.   Yes, little prince, I have one: a garden for you.

FÉLIX.   Let's leave, little Adrián. We have a long way to go before night falls. We still have many miles to cover before reaching the sea.

ADRIÁN.   I don't want to go to the sea.

FÉLIX.   I do. I'll get on one of those big ships that go to faraway countries and they'll never catch me.

ADRIÁN.   The captain'll lock you up alongside the burning boilers and you'll die.

FÉLIX.   No, I won't be locked up. The captain'll let me take care of his monkey, and I'll be happy watching the seagulls from the deck. I'll sing with the sailors.

              (Extending her hands to him.)

MARCONIA.   Don't go! Stay to see my garden. It will be the most beautiful one that you've ever seen. It has a tree that's so big and so symmetrical that every night angels come down to sleep in it. I used to hear how the birds got all excited and said: "The angels are here."

ADRIÁN.	You saw them, the angels?
MARCONIA.	Yes, my little prince.
FÉLIX.	Don't make me laugh. They're cockatoos, the angels, to be able to sleep hanging onto branches?
MARCONIA.	No, they're angels, just angels.
FÉLIX.	Are they monkeys, the angels, to be able to climb trees?
MARCONIA.	They didn't go up. They came down.
FÉLIX.	Did they come down with parachutes?
MARCONIA.	No. Angels don't need parachutes. They don't fall. They simply came down; they descended like sanctuary lamps.
ADRIÁN.	What are angels like, old Marconia?
MARCONIA.	They're made all of fire, like a wheel of light. They're inside the wheel.
FÉLIX.	If they're made of fire they would burn the tree . . .
MARCONIA.	They didn't burn it. Their fire doesn't burn.
FÉLIX.	They were probably glowworms.
MARCONIA.	No, they weren't glowworms; they were angels.
FÉLIX.	They were probably pumpkins with a candle inside.
MARCONIA.	No, they weren't pumpkins.
FÉLIX.	They were probably balloons.
MARCONIA.	No, they weren't balloons.
ADRIÁN.	They were angels, Félix.
FÉLIX.	They weren't anything, because there's no tree here and you have no garden.
ADRIÁN.	Tell me, old Marconia, did the angels tell you that I was a prince?
MARCONIA.	No, they don't talk . . .
ADRIÁN.	And tell me, old Marconia, was the whole tree illuminated with those wheels of light?
MARCONIA.	Yes, my little prince. The whole tree became resplendent. The angels would hang their light . . .
FÉLIX.	Ha, ha, ha . . . ! As if it were an oil lamp . . .
MARCONIA.	Yes, they would hang it, and then extinguish themselves in order to go to sleep. They were white in their tunics and looked slight and small with their wings folded.
FÉLIX.	They were probably apparitions . . . You yourself are an apparition. I'm leaving, old Marconia. I'm not interested in staying here to listen to your stories. I'm leaving for where they can't find me.
MARCONIA.	In my garden they'll never find you; no one will find you.
FÉLIX.	You're crazy . . . There is no garden!

MARCONIA. Wait . . . Wait for the painter to arrive. He'll surely finish his work today . . .

ADRIÁN. Did the painter take the angels too?

MARCONIA. No, the angels left with the birds. But they'll come back.

FÉLIX. I'll go and I'll never come back!

MARCONIA. Why are you in such a hurry?

FÉLIX. Because I don't want to be in the orphan asylum. I don't want them to find me and shut me up in there again. I like to go about freely, to see everything in the world . . .

MARCONIA. Everything in the world is here. Stay with me!

FÉLIX. No, I'm not staying; I don't care about your stories. *(Pointing to the wall.)*

ADRIÁN. What do you have hanging there, old Marconia?

MARCONIA. It's the smock, the one the painter'll put on when he comes to lay out the garden. The keys are below . . .

ADRIÁN. What keys?

MARCONIA. The ones to my gates. There are seven different gates, each one in a single color.

ADRIÁN. Where are the gates?

MARCONIA. In a big wall, very high, that closed off the garden.

ADRIÁN. Did the painter take it too?

MARCONIA. Yes, my little prince. He has to paint it again with the gates. *(Félix, who has listened attentively to their conversation, breaks into loud laughter.)*

FÉLIX. Ha, ha, ha . . . ! Now I really do believe that you're crazy, old Marconia. Ha, ha, ha . . . ! It's possible to lose one key, or seven, or for someone to steal them from you . . . But to keep the keys and lose the gates . . . Ha, ha, ha . . . !

MARCONIA. I didn't lose them, little boy . . . The painter took them.

FÉLIX. Ha, ha, ha . . . ! What a story!

ADRIÁN. Don't laugh, Félix. *(Speaking to Marconia.)* And what were the gates for?

MARCONIA. They're the gates to the marvelous paths, my little prince.

ADRIÁN. And what're they like?

MARCONIA. They're made of wood, each one in a single color. They're set in the wall and all of them have a big lock. Through them one enters the paths of life. *(A traveler enters on the left. He's preoccupied, whistling, and walking quickly.)*

TRAVELER. Good afternoon.

MARCONIA. Good afternoon. *(Turning toward him.)* Where are you going?

(The traveler looks at the old woman and smiles. He makes as if to stop, and after a gesture of doubt continues on his way.)

TRAVELER.   I'm going in search of my love.

MARCONIA.   Wait . . . ! I'll show you the path.

               (The traveler has already disappeared.)

FÉLIX.   *(Smiling.)* Do you have a path for everyone, old Marconia?

MARCONIA.   No, only seven paths, but everyone can enter . . . , everyone looks for some . . .

FÉLIX.   *(Mockingly.)* And they're yours, you made them?

MARCONIA.   No, they're not mine. I know where they are and I have the keys to their gates . . . Only I have the keys.

ADRIÁN.   And there are seven gates . . . ?

MARCONIA.   Seven: one is the gate of Love, another is that of Glory, another is that of Fame . . .

               (To himself, shaking his head.)

FÉLIX.   What nonsense! *(He shrugs his shoulders and speaks to Marconia.)* Your paths will be very boring . . . They don't interest me. May you be very happy with them, with your gates, and with your garden. This time I'm not delaying. Come, little Adrián. Let's leave together . . .

ADRIÁN.   But I don't want to leave. I want to see old Marconia's garden.

FÉLIX.   Don't you understand that she's crazy?

               (Little Adrián seems to hesitate. Then he sits on the bench beside the woman.)

ADRIÁN.   No, I'm not leaving . . . What'll we do if we don't know a single path? I'm staying.

FÉLIX.   *(Raising his arms.)* Suit yourself . . . Stay! When they find you and take you in order to return you to the orphan asylum, don't tell anyone where I went . . .

ADRIÁN.   But where are you going, Félix?

FÉLIX.   You already know. To the sea! *(He turns to Marconia and says with an air of mockery:)* Do you also have the key to the sea, old Marconia, the key of the gate to the sea . . . ?

MARCONIA.   No, but one can reach the sea along all the paths.

FÉLIX.   Along the one to the asylum I'll never reach the sea. That's why I'm looking for my freedom.

MARCONIA.   But I can unlock the gate of Freedom for you. I have that key.

FÉLIX.   Ah, old Marconia . . . ! You're trying my patience. You're the one who should be in the asylum! On the other hand, because of you they're going to take little Adrián back there. It's your fault. You're driving him mad with the garden. He'll stay here and they'll find him . . .

MARCONIA.   No, Félix, nobody will see him, nobody will find him . . .
(Félix shrugs his shoulders and seems tired of arguing. He changes his tone.)

FÉLIX.   Do you at least have something to eat?
(Marconia raises her hands in a desolate gesture and gazes around with a sad expression.)

MARCONIA.   No, I don't have anything to eat. *(All of a sudden she seems to cheer up and joy shows on her face.)* But when the painter comes back, we'll have cherries . . . In the garden there's a beautiful cherry tree and apple tree. The apple tree's still in bloom, but the cherries'll be ripe . . . And if Señora Hortensia passes by, or Señora Elvira, the shopkeeper's wife, they'll be so pleased that I'm showing them my garden that perhaps they'll wish to invite us to have a treat. They'll offer us cake, or the good caramelized fruits that the shopkeeper has in his colored box, in the showcase.
(Félix sighs and speaks to little Adrián.)

FÉLIX.   Give me some of your bread!

ADRIÁN.   And yours . . . ?

FÉLIX.   I'm keeping it for the road. You're staying here and will have cherries.
(Despite Félix's mocking tone, little Adrián begins to undo the straps of his schoolbag; then he sits on the ground, puts it between his knees, opens it, reaches inside, and takes out a round loaf of bread that he breaks in two pieces. He holds one out to Félix and puts the larger piece back into his schoolbag.)

ADRIÁN.   I can't give you more, Félix. All I have left is this piece to share with old Marconia. *(He turns toward her.)* Will you and I eat afterwards?
(Marconia is going to answer, but Félix interrupts her.)

FÉLIX.   Do you have water, old Marconia?

MARCONIA.   No, not here. You have to go to the square. But you'll see . . . the painter's going to put a fountain in the garden, with a big jet of water that will flow from the mouth of a lion.

FÉLIX. *(Mockingly.)* What a beautiful fountain that's going to be, old Marconia . . . ! All right, I'll look for water along the way. Good-bye . . . Listen, couldn't the painter by some chance also put in your head the brains that are missing?

(Félix starts laughing. Old Marconia looks at him without losing her air of happiness. Little Adrián, who has gotten up from the ground and left his schoolbag on the bench, approaches Félix.)

ADRIÁN. You shouldn't say those things; you shouldn't talk to her like that. She's nice to you, invites you to see her garden and eat cherries; she invites you to stay.

FÉLIX. Some invitation! You've gone mad too, little Adrián. I'm sorry for what's going to happen to you . . . But if, for the last time, you don't want to come, good-bye. *(He turns toward old Marconia and bows ceremoniously.)* Good-bye, old Marconia; may you be very happy!

(Marconia gets up and moves toward Félix, who makes as if to leave at the moment in which another traveler enters. Like the first one, he's a young man, with the air of a vagabond.)

TRAVELER. Good afternoon.

(Marconia turns toward him, but nonetheless he does not stop.)

MARCONIA. Good afternoon. Are you looking for something?

TRAVELER. I'm looking for Fortune and Freedom.

(She follows him toward the exit, trying to catch up with him.)

MARCONIA. Those paths don't go together. But wait and choose. I'll open the gate for you . . .

(Félix runs after the traveler and bumps into Marconia, who is returning, disillusioned, to the center of the stage.)

FÉLIX. I'm looking for the same thing as that man. Good-bye. I'm going with him.

(He also exits on the right.)

(Old Marconia returns to little Adrián's side. She seems hesitant for a moment, and finally sits on the bench. Little Adrián, who has also seemed hesitant and surprised, heads toward the exit on the right.)

ADRIÁN. Félix . . . Félix . . . !

MARCONIA. Let him go! Let him go, little Adrián. Let him go . . . He won't hear you.

(Little Adrián returns to Marconia's side and remains standing, looking sad.)

MARCONIA. He won't hear you . . . See, no one wants to hear me either. I ask each and every traveler where they're going and say that I can point out the path to them . . . And they keep going, in a hurry, without understanding that they won't arrive anywhere.

ADRIÁN. Nobody wants to stop at your gates, old Marconia?

MARCONIA. Nobody. Nobody has ever entered through them.

ADRIÁN. Not you either?

MARCONIA. Not me either. The person who enters through one gate can't turn around to come back and has to renounce the others. I spent many years waiting, because it seemed to me that that way, while I waited, all the paths of life were mine. Now I've grown old. I wouldn't dare to choose one.

ADRIÁN. What are the paths, old Marconia?

MARCONIA. The ones that begin at the seven gates. And the seven gates are: Love, Glory, Fame, Fortune, Adventure, Freedom, and Illusion.

ADRIÁN. You know them all?

MARCONIA. Yes, my little prince.

ADRIÁN. Will they be brought to you today . . . ? Will the painter come today, old Marconia . . . ?

MARCONIA. He'll come today or he'll come tomorrow, but he'll come . . . He'll put in grass and on it trees with their green leaves, their white blossoms, and their red cherries, everything bright and clean. He'll put in the big wall, and the gates'll have such beautiful colors that travelers will stop in front of them. They'll say: "Open them, we want to see where they lead." And then I'll answer them: "You have to choose, only one . . ."

ADRIÁN. And do I have to choose, too?

MARCONIA. You do, too. If you want to enter you have to choose.

ADRIÁN. But first we'll help the painter to lay out the garden . . .

MARCONIA. Yes, we'll help the painter. Look, get ready . . . Put on that smock.

(Little Adrián goes over to the wall, stands on tiptoe, and, pulling it toward him, manages to unhook the

	smock. *He spreads it out and looks at it: it's a common mason's smock made of a coarse, faded fabric.)*
ADRIÁN.	*(Showing it to Marconia.)* It's very big.
MARCONIA.	That doesn't matter. Come. I'll roll the sleeves up for you. *(The boy returns to the old woman's side with the smock in his hand. He tries it on. Marconia rolls the sleeves up over his wrists and, seeing that it drags on the ground covering his feet, she ties the two ends at his knees.)*
ADRIÁN.	Shall I also unhook the keys?
MARCONIA.	Yes, unhook them and bring them to me. *(On the wall, hanging from the same nail where the smock was hung, is a thick wire ring with a bunch of rusty keys. Adrián stands on tiptoe again, but the ring is too high for him to reach. He picks up a stick and snags the ring, letting it fall toward him. At the moment that he turns around two police officers enter.)*
OFFICER 1.	Good morning, good woman.
OFFICER 2.	Good morning.
MARCONIA.	Good morning, Officers. Where are you going?
OFFICER 1.	We're going in search of two fugitives.
MARCONIA.	I don't know that path . . . Why are you looking for them? The person who's fleeing should be allowed to flee.
OFFICER 2.	No, the person who's fleeing should be caught. Have you seen two little boys pass by?
MARCONIA.	So many people pass by . . . And I'm so old!
OFFICER 2.	Yes, you are old, but you can see . . .
MARCONIA.	I see and I don't remember. Travelers pass by, townspeople pass by, children pass by on their way toward the school or toward the country . . . They all come and go, come and go . . . And I continue waiting here . . .
OFFICER 1.	Waiting for whom?
MARCONIA.	Does one know for whom one waits when one waits? No, one never knows for whom.
OFFICER 2.	All right. Tell us, Señora, do you remember having seen two little boys dressed in gray tweed uniforms? They would surely have been in a hurry. They may even have asked you for directions.
MARCONIA.	Nobody asks me for directions.
OFFICER 1.	They're two little boys who escaped from the orphan asylum. They're probably lost.

OFFICER 2. We have to find them before nighttime. Try to remember. Have you seen them?

OFFICER 1. They can starve or freeze to death . . .

MARCONIA. It's not cold . . . And won't they have something to eat?

OFFICER 1. They can drown in the river; a dog can bite them; they can be afraid, they're surely very afraid . . . They probably regret having escaped.

OFFICER 2. Tell us, have you seen them . . . ?

MARCONIA. Did they cross through here?

OFFICER 2. We don't know if they crossed through here. We're also searching for them in other places.

MARCONIA. Were they together?

OFFICER 2. Yes, they escaped together.

MARCONIA. And why did they escape?

OFFICER 2. Oh, good woman . . . ! How do you expect me to know that?

MARCONIA. They were probably mistreated.

OFFICER 1. No, they weren't mistreated.

MARCONIA. They must have been sad.

OFFICER 2. *(With a gesture of impatience.)* Why would they be sad? They were there, like many other children.

OFFICER 1. All the children are in a school.

MARCONIA. But there are children who prefer to travel the world.

OFFICER 2. Children can't travel the world alone. There are too many dangers for them.

MARCONIA. For men, too, there are dangers.

OFFICER 1. For men, too. But men know what they're doing . . .
(More impatiently, affecting calm like when one speaks with someone who doesn't understand.)

OFFICER 2. Yes, all right . . . but we're searching for two little boys and can't waste time. Tell us, have you seen them . . . ?

MARCONIA. You say they were together, that they left together?

OFFICER 2. Yes, they were together.

MARCONIA. No, then I haven't seen them . . . I haven't seen two little boys leave together.
(The two police officers exchange glances and betray an expression of doubt.)

OFFICER 1. *(To his companion.)* Neither of the two got left behind. If one had, we would have come across him . . .

OFFICER 2. *(To Marconia.)* Have you seen one little boy pass by, alone?

MARCONIA. One little boy who came by alone . . . ? No, today I haven't seen any little boy come by alone.

OFFICER 2. Let's go. This poor woman is incapable of giving us any information.

OFFICER 1. So . . . don't you want to help us?

MARCONIA. How can I help you . . . ?

OFFICER 2. Leave her alone. We're hanging about too long. Before night falls we must reach the river. They have to be found. Let's go!

(He makes as if to continue to the right. The first police officer hesitates a moment. He points at the open space in the wall.)

OFFICER 1. And behind that wall, are there paths?

(When he turns around to take in the entire stage, he sees little Adrián, who has remained quiet during this time, beside the undergrowth, with the keys in his hand.)

OFFICER 1. Hey! Who's that little boy?

OFFICER 2. Come here!

(He moves toward him. Little Adrián approaches fearfully.)

MARCONIA. That's the little boy who brings the keys.

OFFICER 1. What keys?

MARCONIA. The ones to all the gates . . . the seven keys.

OFFICER 1. The church has that many gates?

OFFICER 2. Is he the sacristan's son?

(He glances again at little Adrián, who looks intimidated, with downcast eyes. He puts his hand on the boy's head and scrutinizes him thoughtfully.)

OFFICER 1. Are you a mason's apprentice?

OFFICER 2. God knows! Let's not waste more time. Let's go. Night will take us by surprise without our having found the fugitives.

OFFICER 1. Perhaps they didn't come this way . . .

OFFICER 2. We'll check as far as the river. If the boatman has ferried them to the other bank he'll tell us. We can't delay any longer.

(Also moving toward little Adrián.)

OFFICER 1. Did you see two little boys pass by . . . ? They would be about your . . .

OFFICER 2. No, somewhat older . . .

OFFICER 1. Somewhat older, dressed in a uniform . . .

(Little Adrián looks at them without answering.)

OFFICER 2. Did you see them?

ADRIÁN.   I arrived a short time ago . . . I bring the keys.

OFFICER 1. You didn't see anyone . . . ?

ADRIÁN.   I saw one man and afterwards another . . .

OFFICER 2. He seems stupid. Let him be. He didn't see anything either. Let's go.

OFFICER 1. Good-bye, good woman.

OFFICER 2. She should also be in an asylum. And for sure this poor little boy, too.

OFFICER 1. *(To little Adrián.)* What's your name? Who's your father?

ADRIÁN.   My father . . . I was told to bring the keys . . .
            (The two officers shake their heads and look at one another.)

OFFICER 1. Good afternoon.

OFFICER 2. Good-bye, Señora . . .

MARCONIA.   Good-bye, Officers . . .
            (Officer #1 makes as if to ask something, but his companion interrupts him by raising a hand.)

OFFICER 2. We're off.
            (Both exit to the right. Old Marconia continues talking to little Adrián as if no one had interrupted them.)

MARCONIA.   Bring the keys. Let's see if all seven are there . . . Yes, they probably are . . .
            (Little Adrián approaches and the old woman takes the keys and starts counting them.)

ADRIÁN.   Those were the police . . .

MARCONIA.   Yes . . .

ADRIÁN.   They're searching for us . . . Will they find Félix?

MARCONIA.   I have no way of knowing.

ADRIÁN.   Tell me, old Marconia, didn't you have a path for the policemen?

MARCONIA.   They don't need any of my paths; they don't wish for any path in order to follow it to the end. They come and go. They'll walk until nighttime and return. Then they'll go to their homes and have a good hot soup.

ADRIÁN.   Won't we have hot soup?

MARCONIA.   Yes, my little prince, we will . . . But look, the first thing we have to concern ourselves with is the keys.
            (She has the wire ring in her lap and is separating, one by one, the keys that hang from it.)

MARCONIA.   You see? There are seven!

ADRIÁN.   No, there are nine . . . There are two more.

MARCONIA.   All right, two more . . . But the seven are here. And I don't remember where these other two are from . . .

ADRIÁN.   One is probably the key to your house . . .

MARCONIA.   No, little prince. I don't have a house.

ADRIÁN.   You don't have a house . . . ? Where do you sleep?

MARCONIA.   You'll see . . . The lady who's the lacemaker has her shop near the market, and she lets me sleep in a big room there that's on the other side of the street, at the back of the patio . . . It's a good room, although a little dark . . .

ADRIÁN.   Will I also be able to sleep there?

MARCONIA.   We'll find a nicer room for you . . . Don't you think we'll find one . . . ? You're a prince!

ADRIÁN.   We can tell the painter to put a house in the garden for us . . . Don't you think, old Marconia?

MARCONIA.   Yes, that's it. We'll tell the painter. When he comes . . . Surely he'll come today . . .

ADRIÁN.   We'll go look for him. Do you know where he lives?
            (Marconia is pensive for a moment, with a doubtful air about her.)

ADRIÁN.   Where does the painter live, old Marconia?
            (She shakes her doubtful air and all of a sudden seems in high spirits and contented.)

MARCONIA.   He must live beside the church, on the square . . . All the important people live on the square!

ADRIÁN.   We'll ask the important people . . . They'll know him, won't they?

MARCONIA.   Oh, yes, they'll know him! For sure he's already done the portrait of Señora Hortensia with her grand shawl . . . and the one of Señora Elvira . . . For sure he goes to the confectionery in the afternoon to have cake and anisette . . . Maybe we'll see him there.

ADRIÁN.   Let's look for him! We'll tell him to finish our garden soon, and to make it the most beautiful garden there has ever been. Listen, we'll tell him to paint the angels' tree carefully, and not to change it, so that the angels will recognize it. We'll also ask him to put a lot of ripe cherries on the cherry tree, and to place flowers of every color alongside the wall, and to have a lot of water flowing from the fountain . . .

MARCONIA.   Yes, don't let him forget the fountain . . .

ADRIÁN.   It should have a big basin, full of green and red fishes.

	Can I ask him to put in a pretty pond with frogs . . . ? Will he want to put it in, old Marconia?
MARCONIA.	Yes, certainly he will. He's a very nice painter . . . And he'll really like painting such a beautiful garden.
ADRIÁN.	What if he can't paint it, old Marconia? Maybe the garden doesn't fit in his house; maybe he had to leave the trees out . . .
MARCONIA.	Everything fits in the painter's house. Everything. He can paint people. He paints ladies with a fan, gentlemen seated in an armchair, and soldiers on horseback . . . And he can paint a lot of people together, a lot, the people who wouldn't fit in the square, and they're all there, inside the picture, with their clothes and their faces, each one in his place . . . And, if he paints someone who's dying, he stays there as if he were alive. And he can also paint the town, with its streets, houses, church, and town hall. He can paint the mountains, the river, and the sea. And there, in his room, everything fits.
ADRIÁN.	The trees, too?
MARCONIA.	The trees, too.
ADRIÁN.	Although they may be very tall?
MARCONIA.	Although they may be the tallest in the world. He can paint even the Sun and the Moon.

(Adrián looks half surprised, half doubtful.)

MARCONIA.	It's true, my little prince. You'll see how he paints our garden . . . !
ADRIÁN.	If the painter is so powerful I'll ask him to make the pond really deep, with so much water that it'll look like a lake. Frogs will jump at the edge . . . You and I will watch how they'll jump! And some tall grass will grow so that dragonflies will settle on it . . . Listen, old Marconia, will I be able to ask the painter to put a rooster in the garden . . . ?
MARCONIA.	It'll crow at night and wake up the angels . . .
ADRIÁN.	It won't wake them up. We'll tell it not to crow until dawn. The angels leave at dawn. Isn't it true that they leave? This way they'll hear the rooster and know that it's daybreak. We'll hear it too . . . I want to have a beautiful golden rooster with a red comb. I'll feed it corn and call it Epifanio. Do you like that name for my rooster . . . ?

MARCONIA.	It's a pretty name. The rooster will be pleased.
ADRIÁN.	And we'll be able to ask the painter to put a blackberry bush right against the wall . . . Don't you like blackberries, old Marconia?
MARCONIA.	Yes, but a rosebush is better . . . Nothing, though, against the wall, nothing that'll cover up the gates . . .
ADRIÁN.	It won't cover them, old Marconia. Let him put in both as decorations.
MARCONIA.	We'll see what the painter says. First we'll have to ask him to put in the house . . .
ADRIÁN.	A house with a big chimney . . . with pots of flowers on the balcony . . .
MARCONIA.	With its kitchen and its woodshed . . .
ADRIÁN.	With an attic and a window in the roof . . .
MARCONIA.	And a big living room where the sun will come in . . .
ADRIÁN.	And when Félix comes we'll invite him to stay. One day he'll return, right, old Marconia?

(*Marconia shakes her head, answering in the negative, and raises her hands.*)

MARCONIA.	He wouldn't want to stay with us, he's following another path. And he won't return, he won't be able to find us . . .
ADRIÁN.	But perhaps he *will* find us . . . I want him to come back, old Marconia. Aren't you sorry that he's getting on a ship and that the captain's locking him up beside the boilers . . . ?
MARCONIA.	Yes, I'm sorry . . . But you see, I told him not to leave . . .

(*Marconia gazes at little Adrián and, on seeing him so saddened, extends her hand to him.*)

MARCONIA.	Yes, when he reaches the river surely he'll turn around. He must be very tired. Surely he'll look for us and remember the place where the garden is . . . Don't get upset. Now you have to think about choosing your gate.
ADRIÁN.	Will you enter with me?
MARCONIA.	Yes, I'll enter with you. I'm very old and wouldn't dare to enter any gate by myself. But with you, yes, I'll enter with you . . .

(*Little Adrián, who had been standing beside Marconia during this conversation, sits on the ground in front of her and puts his arms around her knees.*)

ADRIÁN. Which one will be our gate, old Marconia . . . ? Tell me again the names of all of them.

(Marconia closes her eyes and speaks as if she were reciting.)

MARCONIA. Love, Glory, Fame, Fortune, Adventure, Freedom, and Illusion.

ADRIÁN. *(To himself.)* Which one will be ours? *(To Marconia.)* The last one is the one I like most . . . the gate of Illusion . . . Do you like it?

MARCONIA. Yes, my little prince. It's also the one I like most.

ADRIÁN. We'll choose that one! Will you recognize it? What color will it be painted?

MARCONIA. I'll recognize it! I don't know what color it will be . . . For sure a color like clouds, that has no name, that'll change with the day and the night . . . But I'll know which one it is!

(Adrián, still sitting on the ground, seems to be reflecting; afterwards, with a decisive air:)

ADRIÁN. I want to see the garden every day . . . I want to live in our house . . . And if we enter through that gate we won't be able to leave . . .

MARCONIA. Yes, my little prince. That gate opens onto a path that leads everywhere . . . We'll follow it until arriving here . . . and then we'll find everything much more beautiful . . .

ADRIÁN. Look, old Marconia, what if a lot of people choose our gate and all of them want to live in our garden . . . ? We won't fit in it. The angels will go off in search of another beautiful tree . . . the rooster will also leave, and even the frogs . . .

MARCONIA. My little prince, the person who enters through that gate chooses a path that is only his and for every step taken there is a different path . . . No one will follow ours!

(Adrián, with his hopes built up, stands and extends his hands to Marconia.)

ADRIÁN. Old Marconia . . . Why don't we go now in search of the painter . . . ? We have to see him before night falls . . . Come. We'll ask at the square . . . Surely he'll be waiting for you . . .

MARCONIA. Yes, surely he'll be waiting for me . . . And for you, too.

(She gets up and prepares to follow Adrián.)

ADRIÁN. We'll ask him for our garden . . .

MARCONIA. We'll ask him for the wall and its gates . . . The potter's boy, who rides his donkey loaded down with jugs, will be free now and offer to help us. We'll bring the wall right here . . .

ADRIÁN. We'll position it and open our gate . . . Do you have the key, are you certain you have it . . . ?

(Marconia raises a bunch of keys and examines them.)

MARCONIA. Yes, here it is . . . You see, this very day we'll be able to open it . . . We'll set out on the marvelous path and, upon our return, find our garden . . .

ADRIÁN. Will the painter lay it out in the meantime? Will the potter's boy help him?

MARCONIA. Everything will be in its place . . . Everything will be here . . .

ADRIÁN. Everything? The cherries, the pond, and the rooster . . . ?

MARCONIA. And the house, and the fountain, and the trees . . .

ADRIÁN. Let's go, old Marconia, let's go . . . We'll be able to see everything this very night! It'll be beautiful to take it all in at night, won't it? The moon will shimmer on the pond and the rooster will sleep beside the blackberry bush . . . Maybe we'll meet up with the angels . . . They probably know that the garden has already been painted . . . Everything will be quiet and we'll hear the jet of water flowing from the lion's mouth . . .

MARCONIA. We'll go into the house and make a good fire . . .

ADRIÁN. Let's go, old Marconia . . .

(Marconia holds her hand out to Adrián, and the two head for the opening in the collapsed wall.)

MARCONIA. Let's go. The painter's probably waiting for us . . .

(They exit at the rear.)

(The two police officers, with Félix between them, enter from the right. Officer #2 leads him by the arm. When they come on stage, Félix stops and the police officers stop too. Officer #2 lets go of Félix, who then rubs his arm conspicuously.)

OFFICER 2. Don't rub. I haven't hurt you.

(Félix does not reply. He glances around, trying to locate something.)

OFFICER 2. Let's keep going. We shouldn't stop.

FÉLIX. There used to be a garden here . . .

OFFICER 1. No, not here. You're confusing this place with another one.

FÉLIX. I'm not confusing it. Now it's like this, but before there was a garden. Old Marconia said so.

OFFICER 1. Who is old Marconia?
(Félix shrugs his shoulders in a doubtful manner, and hesitates before answering.)

FÉLIX. I don't know . . .
(Officer #2 takes Félix by the arm again and pushes him.)

OFFICER 2. Let's go.
(Félix points to the back of the stage.)

FÉLIX. There's a path that way . . .

OFFICER 1. What path?

OFFICER 2. There are probably many paths. We're following ours . . .

FÉLIX. Let's enter there, through the wall . . .

OFFICER 2. No. Let's keep on!

FÉLIX. That way we'll arrive sooner . . .

OFFICER 1. No. We'll arrive sooner by taking the streetcar.

FÉLIX. We're in that much of a hurry?

OFFICER 1. You don't think you've detained us long enough? We need to return you to the orphan asylum, and then continue the search for your companion. You'll have to say where you left him . . .

FÉLIX. I don't know . . . We separated. Maybe he went back by himself. He was timid . . .

OFFICER 2. Anyway, let's go.

FÉLIX. I'm tired. I want to sit down on that bench . . .

OFFICER 2. No!

OFFICER 1. You'll sit down at the asylum. You'll be able to rest there.

FÉLIX. I want to get the sand out of my shoes. It's hurting me.

OFFICER 2. Take them off. But quickly . . .
(Félix sits on the bench and begins to untie the laces of one shoe. Then he takes it off and shakes it.)

OFFICER 1. You don't have sand . . .

FÉLIX. Yes, I do. It bothers me.

OFFICER 1. Your feet are swollen, that's what's bothering you. Do you think it's easy to walk for an entire day?
(Félix takes off his other shoe and shakes it out too.)

OFFICER 2. Hurry up. It'll be night soon.

FÉLIX. Wasn't there anyone here when you passed by? Maybe somebody would have given you news of Adrián . . .

OFFICER 2. Don't talk, and finish up.

OFFICER 1. There was only an old woman and a little boy who was bringing keys to her.

FÉLIX. What keys . . . ?

OFFICER 1. How do I know . . . ? Seven keys. He was probably the sacristan's son . . .

FÉLIX. Was he dressed like a sacristan?

OFFICER 1. No, little boy. There isn't a sacristan's outfit. He wore a mason's smock.

FÉLIX. And where did they go?

OFFICER 2. Let's be off.
(He approaches Félix, grasps him by the arm, raises him, and makes as if to begin walking.)

FÉLIX. Just a moment . . . I still haven't tied this shoe . . .

OFFICER 2. If you don't tie it immediately you'll come with your laces loose. And if you don't want to walk I'll tie you with a rope.

FÉLIX. With what rope?

OFFICER 2. I'll tie you with my belt, then I'll drag you and you'll have to walk.

FÉLIX. I can't walk any farther. I'm very tired . . .

OFFICER 2. When we caught up with you you were running like a rabbit. You'd certainly run again if you could escape . . .

FÉLIX. Why don't we go through that gate . . . ?

OFFICER 1. What gate?
(Félix points at the opening in the wall.)

FÉLIX. That one! It's a very pretty path . . .

OFFICER 1. How do you know?

FÉLIX. You can see a lot of trees.

OFFICER 1. I don't see a single one . . .

FÉLIX. A lot of shrubs and plants . . . And you can reach the town . . .

OFFICER 2. We're going to the city.

FÉLIX. And in the town there's a painter . . .

OFFICER 1. In the city there are a hundred.

OFFICER 2. Let's go! Don't get into a discussion with him . . . Move!

FÉLIX. We could wait until nighttime.

OFFICER 1. What an idea! What would we do here at night?
(Officer #2, who during this conversation has been impatient and uninterested in it, speaks to Félix.)

OFFICER 2. That's it! If you don't do as we say, I'm tying you!

FÉLIX. Just a moment, Officer . . . Don't tie me yet!
(Félix, frightened, assumes a supplicating attitude.)

OFFICER 2. Well then, come already. Let's get a move on.

FÉLIX. Just a moment, Officer . . . We could wait to see if little Adrián'll pass by . . .

OFFICER 1. You'll find him at the orphan asylum.

OFFICER 2. Yes, he's probably been caught by now. He couldn't have run more than this boy here.

FÉLIX. I'd like to go through the town . . . Maybe that's where he is.

(The two officers raise him up, each one by an arm, and push him toward the exit.)

OFFICER 2. Little boy, I'm getting tired.

FÉLIX. I really can't walk . . . I'm hungry.

OFFICER 1. You'll eat at the asylum . . . There's nothing to eat here.

FÉLIX. In the town we'll find everything. Señora Hortensia has a confectionery and could invite us to have cake and anisette . . .

OFFICER 1. This boy is crazy. All the children who escape are crazy.

OFFICER 2. No. What he wants is to see if he can trick us and escape again. Don't let go of him.

(He seizes Félix more firmly by the wrist and starts walking.)

FÉLIX. Officer, you're hurting me . . .

OFFICER 2. Well, walk. If you walk I won't have to hurt you.

(Disconsolate, Félix glances around.)

OFFICER 1. Obey! You see that your resistance is futile.

(Félix starts walking between the two officers with his head turned back toward the rear of the stage.)

FÉLIX. Little Adrián . . . !

OFFICER 1. You'll find him at the asylum.

FÉLIX. Old Marconia!

OFFICER 1. This boy is crazy.

OFFICER 2. Come along! Get a move on!

FÉLIX. Little Adrián! Old Marconia . . . !

(They disappear on the left with Félix's calls still being heard.)

END

Bibliography

Primary Texts

Los que se fueron. Barcelona: Planeta, 1957.

El jardín de las siete puertas. Madrid: Doncel, 1961.

Los días de Lina. Madrid: Magisterio Español, 1964.

Víspera del odio. 2d ed. Madrid: Círculo de Amigos de la Historia, 1970. (1st ed., 1958.)

Secondary Texts

Bleiberg, Germán, Maureen Ihrie, and Janet Pérez. *Dictionary of the Literature of the Iberian Peninsula.* Westport, Conn.: Greenwood Press, 1993. Vol. I (A–K), 354–55.

Domínguez Rey, Antonio. "Concha Castroviejo." *La estafeta literaria* 528 (1973): 15–17.

Galerstein, Carolyn. "The Spanish Civil War: The View of Women Novelists." *Letras Femeninas* 10, no. 2 (fall 1984): 12–18.

Translations

Into French: *Los que se fueron,* 1965.

Into Slovak: *El jardín de las siete puertas,* 1973.

Into English: "La tejedora de sueños/The Dream Weaver." In *Conversaciones 3.* Chicago: Great Books Foundation, 2002.